Alphie,

a Yellowstone wolf pup

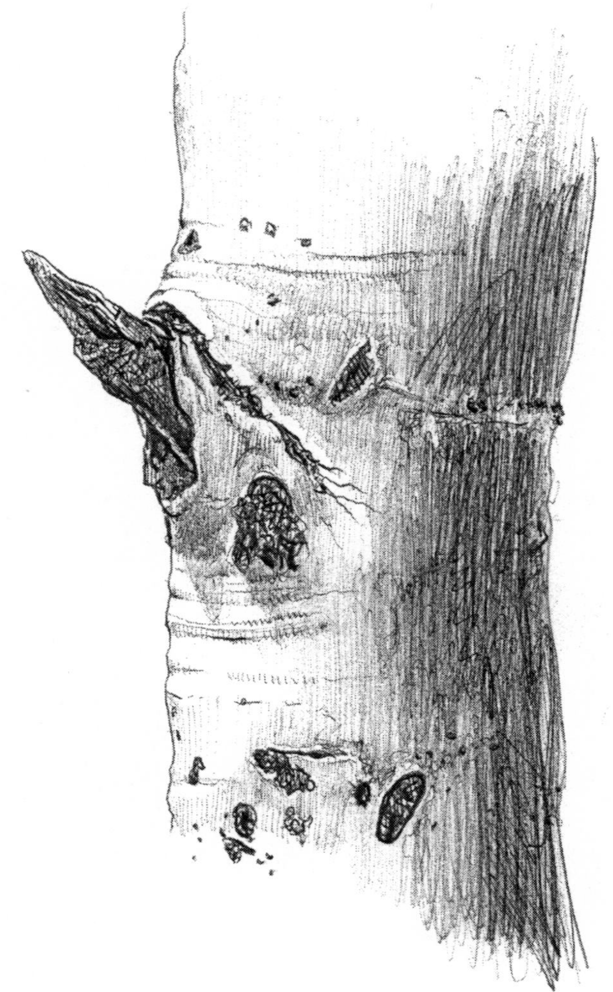

Aging Aspen
4/24/04

CLIFF ON MT NORRIS.

Also by Brian A. Connolly

Wolf Journal, a novel
Wolf Journal, the study guide (Sue Knopp)
Wolftagebuch, German translation of Wolf Journal by Elli H. Radinger
Hawk, a novel, sequel to Wolf Journal
Not Far From Town, short stories & novella
Allegheny River Christmas and Other Stories

Arlie and Papa in Yellowstone, essay written for the Yellowstone Park Foundation (posted on bconnollybooks.com)
The Delisting of Wolf 253M, a YouTube slideshow photo essay

Alphie, a Yellowstone wolf pup, Wolf Journal, Hawk, and Not Far From Town are also available in ebook format from www.bconnollybooks.com., Amazon, iTunes, or Barnes & Noble

Summary

When three month old Alphie, a wolf pup of the Lamar Pack, woke up from a long nap, he discovered that he was alone. His pack had moved to their high country rendezvous at Opal Creek accidentally leaving him behind to face the wild valley on his own. He was lost and frightened. His tiny howls attracted a grizzly and a mountain lion.

After facing many dangers during long days and longer nights, Alphie is rescued by an old wolf returning to the pack. Grandfather becomes Alphie's protector and teacher. Their meeting marks the beginning of a long friendship that weaves its way through all of the exciting adventures that Alphie experiences during his first year as a Yellowstone wolf pup.

Alphie, a Yellowstone wolf pup is a verbal map of the northern range of Yellowstone National Park. Beautifully rendered sketches fill in the details. The story introduces young readers to this special wilderness and wild places in general. Wandering the Lamar Valley, with book in hand, a reader should be able to locate Druid Peak, the Ledge Trail, the rendezvous site, Jasper Bench, Chalcedony Creek, as well as other landmarks in Alphie's territory.

Alphie,

a Yellowstone wolf pup

story by Brian A. Connolly,

sketches by George Bumann

Virtualbookworm.com Publishing
College Station, Texas

Alphie, a Yellowstone Wolf Pup, by Brian A. Connolly
ISBN: 978-1-62137-200-4 (softcover); 9781621372011 (hardcover).

Library of Congress Control Number: 2013901422

Manufactured in the United States of America.

For Sophia, Arlie, and Alyce
in memory of
Hank Gawlowski
&
Wolves 302M & the '06 Female (832f)
-bac

For Mom, Dad, Jenny & little George
-gb

Acknowledgements

Special thanks to Luke, Avery, Jack, Amanda, Ronak, Carter, Gabby, Olivia, Noah, and Erik who, as students in Mrs. Smith's 5th & 6th grade Gifted/Talented Reading Class at Centennial Elementary in Bismark, North Dakota, read a draft of the Alphie stories, first as readers, then as editors. Each of them wrote letters to me, which included excellent editorial comments that altered the presentation of the stories in significant ways. Thank you to them and their teacher, Mrs. Michelle Smith.

Thank you to Kathie Lynch and Mark and Carol Rickman for giving me quiet lodging in Silver Gate where most of the Alphie stories were written. Thank you, too, to Laurie Lyman for patiently answering questions about wolves and young readers, and for keeping me and so many others informed daily about the secret lives of the Yellowstone wolves. I acknowledge that this project would have been much more difficult if it were not for the support of Bill and Cathy Gawlowski, two people who love all things wild, especially wolves. A heartfelt thanks to Dan and Cindy Hartman, great teachers and storytellers. A special thanks to Bill Wengeler for his enthusiastic feedback on the stories. Thank you, also, to Heather Connolly Jerome, one of my main proofreaders and a long time supporter of my writing. Additional thanks to Nate & Trish Connolly who constantly encourage me to keep my pen moving. To Judy Connolly and Kathy Reynolds, a special thanks for helping with all things artistic and grammatical. For her reading and encouragement, a special thank you to Betsy Downy, Wolf Historian. I owe a debt, as well, to Bob Wiltermood for his keen eye for detail and his understanding of wolf biology. To Lena Cochran, for her encouragement and her storytelling, thank you. Thank you to Rick McIntyre, Bob Landis, Carl Swoboda for helping me keep my facts straight and for pointing me in the right direction when wolves were nearby. Finally, a very special thanks to Arlie Connolly who, at age four, inspired these stories with his energetic curiosity about wolves and being lost in wild places.

Author's Notes

As part of the preparation for his bronze sculptures, George Bumann sketches wildlife in his field notebooks. Some of the drawings are quick studies, while others are more complete. Fortunately, many of his sketches were done in or near the Lamar Valley of Yellowstone, Alphie's territory. We decided that rather than produce illustrations that recreate action, we would select sketches that focused on the details of Alphie's world.

In order to have a deep Nature experience, a rich connection to wilderness, it is important to sharpen your powers of observation. The longer you can be still in the woods, the more it will reveal its secrets to you. Using all of your senses will help you to think more deeply about the secrets you are witnessing. One of the objectives of my writing is to help the reader sharpen her/his ability to observe details. George's sketches accomplish the same goal. Studying George's drawings will help you to visualize some of the details of the stories. As you fine tune your senses toward the natural world, you will begin to understand behavior, which, in turn, may lead you to recognize animals as individuals. In so doing, you may be moved to want to protect their habitats, because, at this point, you will feel that the woods, meadows, mountains, and rivers are part of your home, too, a place where you feel welcome, comfortable, and intensely alive.

Wild wolves with radio collars, used in scientific studies, have numbers for names. Some of George's sketches are of Wolf 21M and Wolf 42F, the incredible *alphas* of the famous Druid Peak pack. George and I were privileged to observe the alphas during their long lives, and we honor them here through drawings and by setting the stories in their historic Druid territory, the Lamar Valley.

Italicized words and phrases may be found in the Glossary.

Contents

Part 1
Summer

Alphie, the lost wolf pup of Lamar

Chapter One

The Lamar Valley of Yellowstone is long, wide, and green. The green is sagebrush, buffalo grass, cottonwood trees, willows, and small groves of pale green aspen whose leaves tremble in the slight breeze. The Douglas-fir and lodgepole pine forest is draped like a wool blanket over the lap of the mountains. The Lamar River flows through the valley, a silver snake slithering over rocks in the late summer heat. On the far side of the valley, where *Chalcedony Creek* flows from the high, rocky ledges of Specimen Ridge, a wolf pack sleeps. Though there is nothing to disturb their slumber now, for wolves, trouble can come suddenly like a tornado of teeth and claws in the form of a bear or large cat. Or sometimes it comes in so silently it would not wake a sleeping pup.

The Lamar Pack is snug against the low mounds along the timberline. Mother Wolf looks like a soft, gray rock curled against the black fur of Papa Wolf. Scattered near their parents are two, three, and four year olds as well as several yearlings sprawled out in the intense heat. In a heap by a log is a sleeping pile of puppies worn out from their little wolf games of tug-o-war with an antler, king of the rock, roll-me-over, and hide-n-seek. Alphie, the black puppy with the white crescent moon on his chest, is asleep on a flat rock a little way from his gray brothers and sisters. All six pups are four months old. Above them is deep blue sky cluttered with white cloud ships. Nearby, the river moves like a wind whispering a wolf lullaby.

When Alphie and the other pups no longer needed the den where they were born, the pack brought them here to this *rendezvous* site, a meeting place with water and shade. While most of the adult wolves went hunting for elk, a babysitter wolf stayed with the pups and watched over them as they played and slept. During these hot summer days, the elk leave the Lamar Valley and move into the high country to avoid mosquitoes and flies and to find fresh, green grass. The wolves follow the elk. It was time to move the rendezvous into the mountains now that the elk were grazing so far away.

Mother Wolf woke her mate. Papa Wolf woke the other adults and, finally, the pups.

"It's time to go," Mother barked. "Follow Papa; he knows the way. If we leave now, we'll be at Opal Creek before the moon sets at dawn."

The puppies were confused and sleepy, but they formed a ragged line and followed the long legged adults into the forest. The sun slid toward the western hills, its slanted light turning the rock cliffs copper. The air cooled over the old rendezvous site where insects buzzed, an osprey on the wing whistled, and the scent of sage filled the air.

Chapter Two

Hours passed at the old rendezvous. On the flat rock something dark stirred. It was Alphie! He stretched, yawned, and made a muffled sound while rubbing his eyes with a paw. He sat up slowly and listened. The Swainson's thrush sang his *melancholy* song. A soaring red-tailed hawk called in a raspy voice as his shadow floated over Alphie. A raven clucked from the nearby forest.

Alphie looked around. Mother and Papa were gone; his aunts and uncles were not there; his sisters and brothers were nowhere to be seen. Alphie shook his head to make sure he wasn't having a bad dream. He jumped on a fallen log to get a better view of the rendezvous, but still, the pack was gone.

Alphie searched the beds where the wolves had been sleeping. The smell of wolf was already faint. In the twilight, the little wolf walked the familiar trails along the Lamar River, but there were no fresh tracks, no wolf smells. The black pup began to whimper. A *kestrel* hovered like a colorful kite across the river, and a golden eagle watched the pup's movements from his perch on a dead tree.

Darkness flowed across the sky like black ink spilled on a blue table. Stars appeared, little jewels of light. The only moon in the valley was the white crescent on the small wolf's chest. Its faint glow could be seen above the flat rock where he sat in the dark, alone and frightened.

Alphie put his head back and whispered a baby howl, "Ooohoooooohohoo." So quiet was his voice that he could hardly hear it. “Louder, Alphie,” he said to himself. “Ooohooooooooohohoo!” he sang. His small, quavering voice was so thin in the immense dark. Alphie howled and howled, but got no response. A brown bat flitted by and gave him a scare. A *snipe* bird whistled in the high darkness. A nighthawk called, echolocating his next meal: bezzzer! bezzzer!

Finally Alphie moved like a shadow into the woods where he found his secret place, a small cave among some boulders. He curled in a ball with his big feet sticking out from under him and his thick tail covering his nose. He slept.

As he slept, Alphie dreamed about playing tag with his brothers and sisters. He dreamed about chasing a ground squirrel. His feet twitched and his tail swished as he dreamed. Another dream reached back into a strong memory. It was a recurring dream of his mother in the den. It was so real that Alphie could feel his sisters and brothers pushing against him in order to get closer to Mother Wolf to nurse, could hear them mewing for attention, and could see them shifting their little bodies in the dim light of the den. Then suddenly the dreams were gone, and he was wide awake. A snapping twig brought Alphie to his feet! He was sure the twig was not part of the dream. From the entrance of his cave he could see that the August moon, an ivory stone worn by water, had risen. The woods, perfectly still and full of shadows, were the color of milk.

Alphie listened. He sniffed the air. Lingering there was a smell most foul, some rotten breath exhaled recently in the dark. He looked at the rock and tree shadows. None moved. Then he heard a sound, a snuffling, a pig-like snorting. Something was smelling around near the mouth of the cave.

Suddenly there rose up in front of Alphie a towering shadow that blotted out the moon. The animal had silver tipped fur where the moonlight touched it. When it turned, Alphie could see the massive hump between its shoulders. The grizzly bear roared at the small wolf who tumbled backward into the cave. Alphie hid himself against the back wall of the cave while the bear growled and huffed because he was too big to fit in the entrance. The grizzly reached in and swiped at the pup with big paws and those long claws. He tore at the boulders to enlarge the hole, but they did not budge. A storm of growls and groans filled the cave and shook Alphie, but the wolf pup made no sound. The bear tried pushing his gigantic head into the cave, but only his wet lips and gleaming teeth would fit. His hot breath smelled like worms.

Finally, the bear turned away. Alphie could hear him wandering off through the woods, breaking twigs and muttering to himself. Once the bear was gone, the black pup waited in the gray silence almost afraid to fall asleep because he knew dark dreams waited there. Lost dreams. Bear dreams.

Chapter Three

In the silver light of the Lamar Valley morning, the black wolf pup moved like a small shadow through the sage flats east of the rendezvous site. The air was cool; the sky was blue. Alphie took many steps then stopped, listened, and sniffed the air before moving on. He repeated this pattern all the way to the river.

Alphie heard and smelled the river before he saw it. It sounded like other animals talking and laughing. The Lamar smelled of fish, a hint of *sulfur*, and damp earth. The musty breath of the stream was warmer than the air, which caused wisps of vapor to dance above the dark green water like spirits.

Earlier in the morning when Alphie had been howling for the pack, he remembered his dream of being in the den. Maybe that's where they all went, he had thought. In hopes of reuniting with his family, he had headed toward the old den in the forest on the slope of Druid Peak. Between him and the den lay the sage flats, the Lamar River, and Soda Butte Creek. He worried that the scary grizzly might still be nearby. However, his desire to find the pack was stronger than his fear of the bear.

Now at the river's edge, Alphie lowered his head to drink from the quiet waters of a deep pool. Instantly he jumped back and barked at the black wolf looking up at him from the mirror like surface. He approached the water again, this time with a low growl. The water wolf growled as well. Alphie stomped the wolf with his front paws and was relieved to discover that the other wolf was made of water, a liquid shadow.

He drank deeply, lapping up the water with his pink tongue. While doing so his eyes watched the sky, the cottonwood trees, and the willows floating in the pool. The odd movement that caught his eye was of something dark brown growing larger as it rose from the depths of the pool. Actually the brown feathery *raptor* was falling from the sky, and its shrill whistle nearly turned Alphie inside out! He leapt back toward the safety of the sage just as the osprey hit the water feet first. It was as if the mountain had thrown a boulder into the pool with a foamy spray reaching out toward both banks.

Alphie's heart raced as he watched the large bird flap his dark wings, heave his white chest against the water, and lift his masked face skyward. The bird slowly rose into the air amidst a rainbow spray clutching in his *talons* a cutthroat trout. As the fish hawk gained altitude, it shifted its grasp of the wriggling fish so that the trout faced forward, easier to fly home that way. Alphie remained hidden until the whistling of the hawk faded down the valley.

Now that the drama had subsided, Alphie realized that the river was not as he had remembered it. The water level was low. The rapids above the pool was a mere gurgling compared to the shouting water of early summer when *snowmelt* fed the streams. Alphie was able to cross without the fear of being swept away. He swam across the pool easily and *emerged* on the far bank. There he shook off water creating a rainbow spray of his own.

With his wet fur, the wolf pup looked even smaller as he made his way over a tangle of driftwood logs bleached silver by the sun. Alphie followed a row of cottonwood trees that led him into a thicket of tall willows where strange smells were plentiful and tracks of a dozen sizes criss-crossed in every direction. He passed a wet bison patty imprinted with raven tracks that looked like *fossils* in dark rock.

The voice of Soda Butte Creek was higher pitched than that of the Lamar River. The creek water was faster where it was pinched by steep banks close together. When Alphie came upon the stream, he was startled by an immense beaver who hissed at him and then slapped the water with his flat tail. The clap of sound sent a warning along the creek, and all wildlife went silent. Animals and birds listen to each other in an effort to avoid danger. Once they realized that it was just a wolf pup passing through, they resumed their conversations.

Chapter Four

Alphie worked his way upstream to where the creek widened. The shallow water perfumed the air with its distinct sulfur odor. Alphie remembered the smell and that Mother Wolf had called it 'stink water'. He crossed, shook off, and headed through the dry meadow of sagebrush and brown grasses. The little wolf felt exposed, out in the open, so he hurried along to the steep slope that led up the mountainside to the den forest.

Even though the sun was bright, the forest was dark except for some shafts of light that cut the shade like silver swords. Alphie was moving back along the same trail that had led him away from the den many weeks ago. Memories flooded his small brain. He remembered his brothers and sisters tackling each other and him, the joy of attacking sticks, and the bravery when they would growl down a badger hole.

Alphie's daydream was interrupted when he rounded a fallen log and looked squarely into the empty eyes of an elk skull. He froze for a moment staring at the exposed teeth and the twin branches of the massive antlers. The ghostly head with its awful grin was a *grim* reminder that life in the wild is uncertain, especially for those who are not careful.

Alphie continued on his way. The trail wound through a grove of aspen trees and rose gradually past skinny lodgepole pines and massive Douglas-fir trees. Alphie climbed a sloping boulder and howled. "Ooohooohooohoo!" he called, his tiny voice breaking the silence. He listened for a response, got none, and howled again. A soft wind was pushing against the forest causing the trees to sway just enough so that those that touched one another creaked *eerily*. When you're all alone, Alphie thought, this is a spooky place.

The wolf pup could see larger boulders in a pile further up the mountain. These giant rocks, each the size of ten bears, created caves below them, which is where some of the dens were located. Alphie could see two other den openings that had been dug under the roots of *ancient* Douglas-firs. It was in the biggest of these that he had been born.

Alphie raced up the slope and explored all of the den sites, his small black tail whipping back and forth excitedly. Mother Wolf had moved her pups twice when fleas became a *nuisance*. Alphie found the dens he had occupied and rolled in the dust of each trying to recapture the smell that was so familiar to him. He felt comforted by his memories, the dusty odors, and the many toys he had found like the ones Papa Wolf had brought to the rendezvous.

One toy was a shed blacktail deer antler used for tug-o-war. It was covered with tiny teeth marks made by wolf pups. There were also scrapes where porcupines had gnawed on the *tines*. Alphie picked up the antler and headed down the trail toward the valley. He had not found his pack, but did find comfortable memories and an old toy.

As he passed through the forest, Alphie held his head high so that the antler would not drag on the ground. Several times it thumped against trees. The willows along the bank of Soda Butte Creek posed a problem. The tines kept hooking on branches. Alphie found that by walking backwards dragging the antler, he was able to get it to the creek.

The wolf pup was about to have another lesson on the fact that Nature consists of *tranquil* periods of calm interrupted by intense drama. Half way across the creek, he found himself in the middle of a drama that had started moments earlier. The little wolf with the antler in his teeth looked upstream when he heard several splashes. Running downstream was a small moose calf followed by its very large mother. The calf had rusty-brown fur; the mahogany fur of the mother was almost black. They appeared like logs moving through water on bony legs. Their long faces bobbed as they ran. Their eyes were wild. The animals moved in a constant spray of exploding water.

Alphie dropped his antler toy, which tumbled away in the current and was gone. The moose were nearly upon him by the time he made it to the far bank. There he hid behind a fallen log surrounded by willows. He watched as the moose thundered past. No sooner had they disappeared downstream than the coyotes appeared upstream. On opposite sides of the creek, they were running along the banks.

All of their senses were focused on the moose until the one nearest Alphie ran through the invisible scent trail the wolf pup had left behind. The coyote stopped suddenly, sniffed one way, and then the other. She was the color of fall wheat with some dark hair woven in along her back. The backs of her pointed ears were rusty brown, and her long muzzle showed bared teeth as she growled in Alphie's direction.

At that moment Alphie heard more commotion coming upstream. Both wolf pup and coyote turned to see the angry cow moose chasing the male coyote. Her calf was at her heels crying and stumbling to keep up. The wet fur of both glistened in the bright sunlight. The cow kicked forward with her long legs sending the squealing coyote head over heels. The coyote regained his feet and limped into the willows.

Without hesitation the cow turned her attention to the other predator, the female coyote. She crossed the stream in two long steps and reared up to stomp the coyote. The coyote flattened her ears, a sign of fright, turned, and dashed upstream just as the great hooves of the cow hit the muddy spot where the coyote had been. Some of the mud splashed on Alphie. Satisfied that the coyotes had given up the chase, the cow pranced downstream with her calf practically under her.

Once the drama had ended, Alphie continued on his way back to the rendezvous. He crossed the Lamar River without incident, but moved through the sage flats with his head hung low. He had not found his pack. The antler toy was lost. He was wet, tired, and hungry. He did eat a large, black beetle, but it tasted nasty and wiggled a lot.

By late afternoon, Alphie had made it back to the rendezvous site. He curled up on his flat rock and slept until dark. Then he dragged himself through milky moonlight to his secret cave where he slept through a night filled with dreams of being chased by angry moose and coyotes.

Chapter Five

In the morning when gold sunlight flooded the Lamar Valley, Alphie returned to his flat rock. The moon had fallen into the forest. Paintbrush flowers, *harebells*, and sagebrush dripped with dew. The meadowlark was whistling in the new day. A Peregrine falcon on the hunt shot across the sky like a feathered star.

Alphie began to howl again, hoping his parents would hear. "Ooohoooohoohooooo!" The small herd of bison by the river heard. The coyotes near the cottonwood trees heard. The blacktail deer on the hill heard. Even the bluebirds in the aspen grove could hear the faint voice of the wolf pup in *distress*.

"Oohooooohohooo," howled Alphie. Then he listened for a reply. None came. "Oohooooohohooo," he cried again. Still no reply. All the long day he howled and listened. He made one trip to the river to drink, but was chased by a badger, scolded by a *marmot*, and almost stepped on by a bison who snorted at the pup.

A ground squirrel, fat and slow, moved in the grass near Alphie's flat rock. Quick as lightning, Alphie pounced. He savored the taste of the delicious squirrel. Later he caught grasshoppers and a beetle, but shuddered as he swallowed the awful tasting *delicacies*.

Late in the afternoon clouds grew into dark cliffs and erased the sun. The hail came first like a shower of stinging pellets, white ice that shredded plants. Alphie took shelter in his cave. Lightning flashed, and all the dark places danced with light. The cannon fire of thunder crashed among the high cliffs of Specimen Ridge causing an *avalanche* of sound to tumble into the valley. The small wolf shivered in his cold cave and clenched his whole body when thunder shook the earth. He felt the heartsick fear that comes from being lost and alone in a dark, stormy world. Alphie listened to the hard rain, and before he could count to ten, he was asleep.

© '02

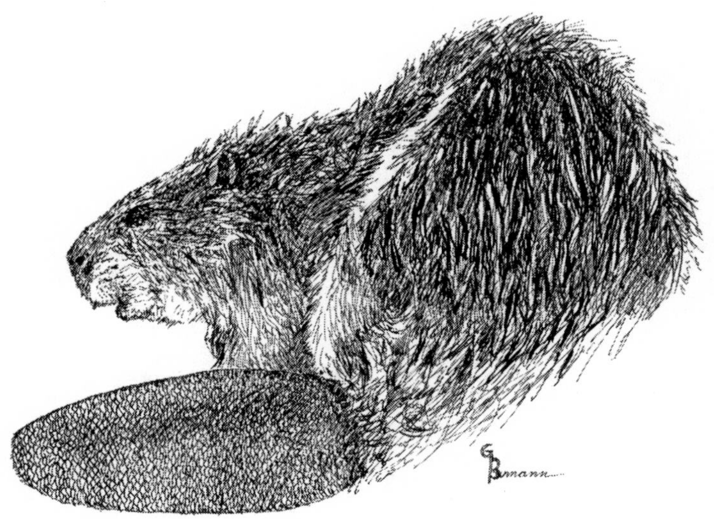

MOOSE STUDIES
MARCH 8, 2006

Chapter Six

When Alphie awoke the following morning, he discovered that the valley was bejeweled with raindrops glistening in the sun. They hung gold and silver from every blade of grass, every wild blossom, every cluster of needles on drooping pine *boughs*.

Alphie's morning went well until a mountain lion tiptoed out of the woods. The tawny brown cat, as big as a full-grown wolf, had a round, whiskered face and a long tail that followed her like an undulating snake.

A wolf's sense of smell and hearing are excellent, but their eyesight is average. At a distance, they have difficulty recognizing other pack members. At first Alphie thought the lion was his mother returning for him. He howled his delight from his flat rock. "Ooohooooohoo!" The big cat stopped mid-step with one paw raised. As the cat's yellow eyes focused on the black animal on the rock, a smell came to Alphie that was not wolf. The strange odor set off an alarm in him. He sprinted toward the forest and the safety of his cave.

At the same moment, the cat extended her sharp claws and jumped into the air toward Alphie. Two leaps, and the lion was right behind the fleeing wolf. Alphie heard sticks crack to his right, so he dashed left. He was almost to his cave when the cat's paws landed on either side of Alphie. His little wolf heart jumped!

Suddenly the mountain lion yelped and rolled sideways into a sage bush. From his cave, Alphie could hear more yelps, as well as growls and barks. He heard the loud cry of the cat as it ran off into the deep woods. It was then that Alphie smelled wolf.

Chapter Seven

Alphie poked his head out of the cave into the bright sunshine to see if the danger had passed. The smell of wolf was strong. Bedded in the shade of a tall lodgepole pine was a slate gray wolf. He nodded at Alphie and said, "Good morning, little wolf."

"Who are you?" asked Alphie.

"I'm the one who saved you from the lion," said the big gray.

"But you are not a Lamar Pack wolf," Alphie said.

"I was once, a long time ago," the wolf said. "When I was born, I was midnight black just like you. But now that I am old, my fur has turned gray. Look at this." The old wolf stood so that Alphie could see his slate colored chest. There, faint as candlelight, was a crescent moon just like Alphie's.

Alphie whispered, "You are the Old One my parents speak of!"

The old wolf smiled. "I prefer to think of myself as your grandfather," he said as he bedded once again.

Alphie's eyes grew wide with excitement. He ran to the old wolf, crawled over his back, jumped on his head, and licked his face in greeting. It was then that Alphie saw the blood on Grandfather's left shoulder.

"You're bleeding, Grandfather!" he cried.

"It's just a scratch. It'll be sore for a day, but we will still be able to go in the morning."

Alphie looked puzzled. "Go? Go where?"

"To Opal Creek up on Mirror *Plateau*. Our high country rendezvous is there. We have used it for many years in the late summer.

The pack follows the elk there when they leave the valley for the mountains."

"Is it far away?" Alphie asked.

"Not so far as the wolf walks or the raven flies, but far enough that your momma and papa cannot hear your howls." The old wolf licked some blood from his shoulder and continued, "I know this because when I was a pup like you, almost ten years ago, I, too, was left behind."

"You were lost?!" asked Alphie.

The Old One thought for a minute, and then answered, "I wasn't really lost because I knew where I was, right here, but I was lost without my family. They always fed and protected me. Without them I was frightened by bears, threatened by mountain lions, bison, and even coyotes."

"What did you eat when you were lost, Grandfather?" Alphie asked.

"Ground squirrels and grasshoppers." Grandfather licked his lips.

"Me, too, but, Grandfather, I don't like grasshoppers. They're nasty! Yuck! And I ate a large beetle that I forgot to chew like momma always says. So he wiggled and tickled all the way down my throat. It was awful! No more bugs!"

Grandfather laughed. "I have some real food *cached* nearby. We'll eat elk tonight!"

When darkness settled on the valley like a soft blanket, Alphie curled himself against Grandfather. One of the old wolf's huge paws served as a pillow. Alphie felt safe and warm. He fell into a deep sleep and dreamed of being an older wolf chasing elk through the valley. He whimpered softly, and his feet twitched as he dreamed.

Chapter Eight

A deep voiced howl startled Alphie awake. The sun was balanced on the top of Mount Norris, and the valley was bursting with light. "Ahhhoooohooooohooo!" howled Grandfather. He looked at Alphie. "I'm trying to get a response from the family."

Alphie, sleepy eyed, listened for a reply. He heard the flute like voice of the western tanager singing along the edge of the forest. Sandhill cranes, feeding on the hillside, gave their harsh call. A pair of coyotes yipped and barked near the river. An osprey and a bald eagle screeched in mid-air where they fought over a cutthroat trout. However, there was no answer to Grandfather's howl.

"If they aren't going to find us," said Grandfather, "we'll have to find them. Follow me."

Grandfather set off across the field heading south. Alphie followed. The old wolf took big steps with his long legs. The young one had to run to keep up. Where the Chalcedony Creek Trail started up the mountainside, the pup looked back at the rendezvous site that had been his home for so long. He was sad to leave his secret cave, the flat rock, the antler toys Papa had carried home. It was a comfortable place. He was about to turn back when Grandfather said to him, "Did I tell you that the whole pack will return here when the snow begins to fall in the mountains? The elk winter here. We follow the elk."

Grandfather's words comforted Alphie. The two wolves continued into the pine forest and up the mountainside where a great horned owl watched them pass. On the Specimen Ridge Trail Alphie climbed onto a fallen tree made of stone, a petrified tree. He could see across a high meadow to Mount Norris, a peak across the valley where bighorn sheep lived. To the south he could see Cache Creek, a place where many of the family stories happened. It was where Papa had been born.

Grandfather pointed north to the Den Forest spread below the cliffs of Druid Peak where he and Alphie were born. Alphie told Grandfather about his adventure returning to the den. Grandfather said, "You are a brave wolf to travel so far from the rendezvous alone. It's dangerous for a small wolf."

"I know that now," said Alphie.

Also visible was Soda Butte Creek, which flowed into the Lamar River, where one of Grandfather's sisters was lost downstream in fast water during the *Crossing*. From where they stood, they could see the little volcano, Soda Butte Cone, from which the stink water flowed.

Alphie asked about the Crossing. The old wolf sat on the stone tree next to his grandson and explained. "As you know, when puppies are weaned, done nursing," he said, "they no longer need the den. They are too big for such a small space. So your parents led you, as they were led when they were pups, to a rendezvous site. For our pack that has meant crossing two streams full of snowmelt: Soda Butte Creek and the Lamar River. They are still full of fast water in July. It is dangerous for pups who have to swim swift water."

Grandfather looked at the distant streams, two ribbons of sky, and thought about when he was a young wolf. Even though he knew the water was low now, Alphie remembered his own Crossing just a month ago. He had been so frightened by the dark water that Mother Wolf had to carry him across in her jaws. It felt good to think about his mother. Alphie put his head back and gave an exuberant puppy howl. "Oooohoohoo!" Grandfather howled as well in a longer, deeper voice. "Ahoooooohooooohoooho!" he sang. The pair sat in silence for many minutes. They looked at each other when they heard a distant sound, like an echo. It was another wolf voice coming from far to the south, deep in the Mirror Plateau where Opal Creek flowed. The howl was as faint as thought. Grandfather howled again, and the same voice was carried back to them on the wind.

Chapter Nine

Grandfather and Alphie headed south toward the voice. They moved into a forest of dead trees, ones, still standing, that had been burned in the *Great Fire*. Many of the bare branches looked like bones and had emerald green moss hanging from them like loose skin. Small lodgepole pines had begun to grow because the heat from the fires opened the cones releasing the seeds. It takes fire to grow some trees. Many of the dead trees had fallen over so that the forest floor looked like a giant game of pick-up-sticks. Grandfather stepped over most of the logs while Alphie ducked beneath ones that were stacked above the ground. Several times in this *maze* of sticks, the small wolf lost sight of Grandfather. The big wolf whose slate gray coat matched the color of the dead tree trunks would woof to let the pup know his location.

As they moved through the burned land, a robin barked an alarm, chipmunks scurried for holes in fallen logs, a pine marten watched from its nest of mistletoe, and a raven eyed them as it hopped and flapped from tree to tree squawking as it moved.

Grandfather stepped cautiously into a *boggy* meadow and halted. Alphie stood under his grandfather peering out between his tall legs. A chorus of short, high pitched howls and barks sounded from the far side of the meadow. Grandfather stiffened.

"What is it?" asked Alphie.

"Coyotes," he replied, displeased with himself that he hadn't smelled them first.

Even though the small *canids* were only a third the size of Grandfather, the two coyotes charged across the meadow toward the large wolf. Grandfather lowered his head close to Alphie and whispered, “Wait here.”

The old wolf raised his tail high, an *alpha sign*, a sign of dominance, and raced toward the challengers. They, in turn, nearly turned inside out trying to reverse their direction. Within seconds Grandfather was on them. He rolled them over and bit each one on the tail. They squealed their pain and ran across the meadow as if their fur was on fire.

Grandfather sauntered back to where Alphie stood in the grass. Alphie’s thick tail wagged. He greeted Grandfather by licking his face and rubbing his tiny body against the old wolf's long legs.

Chapter Ten

The two wolves continued south skirting the meadow and entering a large stand of woods, which had been spared by the Great Fire. The tall pines grew close together turning day into night. Alphie did not like the spooky sounds he heard: trees creaking as they rubbed against each other; the swoosh-swoosh of the wings of a gray, silent bird; and the muffled voice of the wind.

Grandfather stopped, sniffed the air, and said, "Bison."

And, sure enough, in a clearing just a little way down the trail stood a large bull staring at the two *intruders*. The bull's head alone weighed more than Grandfather. The *coarse*, black wool of his *mane* covered his huge head, his massive shoulders, and his front legs. His hips and hind legs had very short fur that exposed his powerful muscles. The bison shook his head and beard, and stared at the wolves with dark eyes. His short tail, with the tuft of fur on the end, was raised showing that he was angry that these *trespassers* were in his woods. He drooled strings of green saliva. Disgusting, thought Alphie. Thunder shook the trees when the bison bellowed his displeasure.

Grandfather grinned. "I know this bully bison. We've met before. He's big and dangerous, but slow. While I distract him, Alphie, you circle around. I'll catch up shortly."

Alphie moved off the trail and disappeared. The bison rolled in a dusty *wallow*. He stood and scratched the dirt with his hooves. He then thrashed a sage bush with his great head and horns. Part of the bush broke loose and clung to his horn like a decoration. Grandfather charged straight at the bison, snarling as he moved. The bison was surprised by the courage and speed of the old wolf, and stumbled backward several steps. Grandfather was a gray streak passing the beast, nipping one of its legs. The bison jumped at the sudden pain, and whirled around swinging his horns at where the wolf had been. Then he looked both ways and saw no wolf. Grandfather had already circled behind him and nipped the bison on another leg. The bison jumped again and tried to stomp the old wolf into the ground, but grandfather was already gone.

From down the trail Grandfather and Alphie could see the bison jumping around looking for Grandfather, expecting to be bitten again. The two wolves laughed and laughed as they moved on through the woods.

Chapter Eleven

Grandfather led the way down a trail as ancient as time. Wolves had used it for thousands of years. For a while it became overgrown and was almost lost. That was during the long decades of the *Disappearance* when wolves were gone. But then, a few generations back, they returned. Even though there was no memory of the old trails, the new wolves that came to Yellowstone soon found the same paths used so long ago.

As Grandfather loped across No Name Creek and into another burn from the Great Fire, he told Alphie the stories of the first wolves, the Disappearance, and the return of the wolf. Grandfather explained that his own grandfather had been the first wolf to come back to Yellowstone, the first wolf to discover this trail, the first wolf in many years to fill the valley with his howling.

Grandfather told about the time when the mountains cried. Because the wolf was gone, elk, bison, and deer ate all the grasses and new trees. The birds left; the beaver disappeared; the creeks and rivers grew heartsick. Coyote tried to fill the wolf's paws, but he made a mess of things. It was a dark time for the Lamar Valley.

"But now we wolves are back," said Grandfather. "You have seen the beaver building his lodge, the warbler birds their nests. The aspen trees once again dance in the wind, and the coyote is pleased to have his old job back. We have restored balance to the valley. If you listen very closely on a quiet evening, you can hear the harmony of all things, and you will know that you are part of that wilderness song."

Chapter Twelve

As Grandfather finished his last sentence, he stepped into a wide clearing of tall grass. Alphie jumped up on a stump in order to see across the field. On the far side stood a large, black wolf. His yellow eyes were locked on Alphie and Grandfather. Alphie was certain that they had found Papa Wolf, his father. The little wolf put back his head and howled as loud as he could. "Ooohooooohoo!"

Grandfather reached a large paw over and covered the small wolf's muzzle. Alphie looked at him questioningly. "What's wrong, Grandfather?" he mumbled.

"This wolf does not smell right. He's not from the Lamar Pack. He's a stranger."

Grandfather moved a few steps closer to study the black wolf. He was a young wolf, but very big and muscular. He held his tail high, the alpha sign. Finally Grandfather recognized Big Black from the Pelican Creek Pack. This wolf had come into the Lamar Pack territory to cause trouble. It was possible, thought Grandfather, that there were more wolves just out of sight. Big trouble, he thought. If they meant to take over the territory, they would wipe out Grandfather and the little black pup.

Grandfather pushed Alphie gently to the ground. "Stay," he said. "When the fight begins, run like the wind away from this place. Don't look back. Find family."

"But, Grandfather," Alphie protested.

"Remember your grandfather," he said, "and grow up to be a great alpha of your own pack. Tell the family that the Pelicans are near. They'll know what to do."

Grandfather moved slowly toward the center of the field. Gold, blue, and pink wildflowers gave off their powerful perfume. Grandfather knew he had no chance against such a strong wolf, but perhaps he could buy Alphie some time to get away and find the pack.

Big Black moved toward the old gray wolf giving out a low growl and baring his white teeth. Behind the black wolf, two gray wolves stood up from where they had been bedded in the tall grass. They began moving slowly toward Grandfather. The old wolf rose up on his hind legs and bark howled, half bark, half howl, to warn off the approaching wolves. They kept advancing toward him, their heads low, their voices threatening. Once again Grandfather rose up and bark howled in a deeper, more serious voice.

Big Black and the two grays stopped. Grandfather barked again. The three wolves took several steps backward. Feeling more confident, Grandfather snarled and lunged at the wolves. All three turned, tucked their tails, and ran for the woods.

Grandfather grinned. "I guess I showed them," he said to the wildflowers.

When Grandfather turned around to look for Alphie, he discovered the Lamar Pack, all twelve adults, standing in a line behind him! Alphie, followed by his sisters and brothers, ran through the tall grass to Grandfather. The six pups swarmed over the old wolf giving him kisses, licks, rubs, and little puppy love bites. The adults joined the welcome home for the lost puppy and his Grandfather. They formed a huge wolf pile so that it was difficult to tell where one wolf ended and another began. They *jawed*, wriggled, rubbed, and nuzzled each other for many long minutes. Then the wolves sat facing all the directions and howled their wild joy at having Grandfather back with them and having their lost puppy home. "Ahoooohoooooohooohooooooohoo!" they sang. And the loudest voice of them all was Alphie's, no longer the lost pup of Lamar.

Part 2
Fall

Alphie Returns to Lamar Valley

WOLF 21

Chapter One

High on the Mirror *Plateau* on the bank of Opal Creek, Alphie lay curled up against Grandfather Wolf. It had been very cold during the night. The black wolf pup was *absorbing* body heat from the old gray. However, something icy was tickling his nose. He twitched and covered his muzzle with a paw. Something cold tickled his ears. Alphie rubbed his ears and half opened one eye. Grandfather was white! Alphie was white! "What's this?" he said aloud.

Alphie uncurled himself and sat up. He kept blinking his eyes in order to make the white world around him go back to the way it had been when he had fallen asleep the night before. The white would not go away. The ground was covered with the white stuff. The branches of sage were like paws holding white powder. Even the trees were dressed in ivory colored robes.

The wolf pup stood and shook as if he had just emerged from water. Alphie had grown considerably since his days at the Lamar rendezvous. Even though he was still a pup, he was half the size of the adults. Tall guard hairs stood up along the back of his neck. At fifty pounds, he was larger than his *siblings*. The sugary spray landed on Grandfather, but he did not stir. Alphie saw that he himself was black again except for the crescent moon on his chest. He was still alarmed because his whole world had changed. All the sleeping adult wolves and puppies along the stream were white. The edges of Opal Creek were made of glass, and the very water itself was exhaling steam that rose like gray ghosts wandering along the stream bank. The moving water gurgled under a lip of ice. The sky was low and gray as smoke.

Alphie leapt on Grandfather. “Get up! Get up!” he cried.

Grandfather harrumphed a few times clearing his throat, repositioned his paws under him, and, without opening his eyes, said, “Alphie, go back to sleep. It’s too early.”

“But, Grandfather, look!” he cried, his voice filled with *anxiety*.

Grandfather lifted his head and looked around. He smiled. “Oh,” he said, “it snowed. No wonder you’re upset. You’ve never seen snow before. Don’t worry, little one, you are made for snow.” The old wolf sat up. “This is what winter looks like. Your coat is already getting thicker to keep you warm. And look at those big feet of yours! You were born with snowshoes. Snow is great for playing wolf games. Why don’t you wake the other pups and show them your surprise. Let Mother Wolf and Papa sleep. They were out late hunting. Cobalt and some others have yet to return.”

Alphie waded through chest deep snow across the small clearing to where Obsidian, Basalt, and Slate, his brothers, and Lupine and Yarrow, his sisters, were sleeping, a circle of white bumps under the snow. Here and there an ear or paw was visible. Alphie plowed right into them shouting, “Get up! Get up!”

The five pups sprang to their feet and looked in all directions for trouble. As amazement swept across their faces at the white world, they instinctively shook snow from their fur. The sisters and Obsidian had dark gray fur with silver along the low sides and bellies, while Basalt and Slate had dark saddles with rusty colored fur blending to blond on the bellies. Both of their tails were cream colored with black tips.

While dancing around the sleepy group, Alphie said, “It’s okay. Grandfather called it snow. He said it’s for playing in. Let’s go climb the rock!”

All six pups raced for the woods kicking up a trail of snow dust behind them. Lupine and Yarrow tackled Alphie causing him to roll in the snow. Obsidian, Basalt, and Slate made it to the puppy rock first. Slate tried to climb the large, flat rock but slid off onto his back. Obsidian leapt on him. Slate began licking his brother’s face. Basalt ran round and round trying to catch his tail. Alphie and his sisters chased each other around the rock a half dozen times. The brothers joined the chase. Several kept biting clumps of snow, which made them appear as if they had sugar on their lips.

Alphie was the first to climb the slippery rock. The others followed. They took turns head butting each other off the rock, squealing as they fell into the trampled snow below. Alphie spied a low hanging pine bough heavily *laden* with snow. He jumped and jumped trying to bite the branch. Finally, he grabbed the branch in his teeth and was instantly covered by a small avalanche of snow. For a moment he hung suspended above the rock, above the others with his legs dangling down. He did not want to let go. When he did let go, Alphie fell like a pillow on top of his admiring brothers and sisters.

Chapter Two

While the pups were unscrambling themselves on top of the rock, they heard a howl coming from the woods on the far side of Opal Creek. More howls joined the first voice. All the sleeping adults, including Grandfather, *roused* themselves and shook snow from their fur. They answered the howls with a group howl of their own. "Ahoooohooohoo!" The individual voices rose and fell. The puppies joined in as well. Their small voices were sharper and their howls shorter, but their *enthusiasm* was as great as the grown ups. "Ooohooohoo!" they sang.

Mother Wolf said to Papa, "It's Cobalt returning from the hunt."

Four wolves, three grays and a black, burst from the woods, leapt the partially frozen creek, and greeted the other adults with much tail waging and body rubbing. Cobalt, the three-year-old black wolf with a dash of white on his chest, dropped a slab of meat for Mother Wolf and Papa, the *alpha* pair, to eat. The puppies ran to the newcomers and excitedly licked the hunters' faces. The licking triggered *regurgitation.* Each wolf lowered his head and threw up a slightly digested elk stew. The pups *pounced* on the meal chewing, slurping, growling, and pushing. Some stepped in the stew and licked their paws, while others licked their siblings' faces for the *meager morsels* left there.

Cobalt said to Mother Wolf and Papa, "The elk do not like this snow. It covers the grass. Many have already gone down to the valley where the snow has yet to fall. That is where we got the old bull. We should move back to the Lamar rendezvous soon."

Alphie looked up from his meal. He had snow on his nose and elk stew on his chin. He thought to himself, 'Grandfather had said we would go back to the rendezvous in the valley and now the time is here.' He remembered his secret cave in the rocks. He recalled the antler toys, the song of the river flowing over rocks, and the shifting winds each with its own wild odor. He thought about the comfort and safety of the Lamar Valley, his first home.

Papa began howling to rally the pack, get them excited about leaving Opal Creek and returning to the heart of their territory, the Lamar Valley. Mother Wolf and Cobalt howled, as did the others. All moved closer to the alphas, even the pups who raised their heads and added their voices to the song of the wild. As the howling diminished, the pack rubbed, licked, and jumped on each other. The singing and touching strengthened the *bonds* of the family.

Alphie was the first to break from the huddle. He headed across the meadow on the trail home. Near the woods he turned and looked back at the pack. When he saw that the others were not following him, he yelled out orders, "Let's go! Let's go!"

"Hush up!" Mother Wolf barked with her tail raised high, one of the alpha signs. "Puppies do not give the orders in this pack! Papa and I give the orders, and we will continue to do so! Do you understand my words, Alphie?"

"Yes, Mother. I'm sorry," Alphie said with his head low, his eyes *averted.* Papa, with his tail raised, too, snarled at Alphie and pinned him to the ground using his powerful jaws. This was Papa's way of letting the pup know that Mother's words were serious words and that Mother and he were in charge.

Mother Wolf turned to the others and said, "Okay, let's go! Don't leave anyone behind this time."

Alphie looked at Grandfather. Grandfather just grinned and fell in line behind the six pups as they headed north on the trail to the Lamar Valley.

Chapter Three

Even though Mother Wolf and Papa led the pack through the forest, Cobalt and some yearlings spread out to the right and left, like *sentries*, giving the pack a greater view of the *terrain*. The troop crossed No Name Creek. They sniffed the tracks of other animals: elk, bison, coyote, red fox, pine marten, and bear.

The trail brought back memories for Alphie. Thoughts passed through his mind like pictures in a photo album: Big Black of the Pelican Pack, the bully bison, the angry coyotes. He thought about how Grandfather had rescued him and brought him back to his family. As Druid Peak and the *confluence* of the Lamar River and Soda Butte Creek came into view, Alphie recalled the stories Grandfather had told him about the Disappearance, the Great Fire, and the Crossing.

Other memories began to race through Alphie's mind: the old rendezvous, eating bugs, the storm, and the bear. The faster the memories came to him, the faster he waded through the deep snow. Before he knew it, Alphie was way out in front of the pack.

"Oops," he whispered to himself. "I'm supposed to stay with the other pups, but they are so slow. Don't they realize that we are going home?" He waited a minute and then shouted, "Hey, guys! Hurry up! See who can catch me!"

The adults tried to keep the other pups in line, but it was useless. Alphie saw that they were running after him. He turned and ran without looking.

Mother Wolf barked at Alphie, "Alphie, don't...", but he had already disappeared over the edge of a steep ravine. The wolf pup began to slide on his belly with his four legs sticking out in four directions. His big feet stirred up the white powder so that it rose like a white fog behind him. His speed increased as he glided over the snow. Alphie's eyes were full of fear as he hit a snowy log, which *catapulted* him into the air. Whomp! He hit a pine bough, which dropped him head first into a snowdrift.

By the time Alphie had pulled himself from the snow and shook off, the other pups were at the rim of the ravine laughing. At first Alphie was embarrassed, but then he had an idea.

"Hey," he called to them, "you should try it! It's fast and fun! Come on down!"

The pups looked at one another, and then, before the adults could get to them, they jumped over the rim and slid down the snowy slope giggling all the way. They spun and tumbled as they descended. At the bottom they all looked like snow wolves. They jumped each other and swallowed mouthfuls of snow. Alphie pinned Obsidian and Slate on their backs and then gently held Lupine against the snow with his jaws. Yarrow and Basalt bumped Alphie into the snow and licked his face. Through play, the pups were already competing for their places in the pack. Some would become leaders, others followers.

Alphie had just said, "Let's slide down again!", when they heard Mother Wolf growl from above. Grandfather was smiling next to her. Quickly the wolf pups scrambled up the ravine and fell in line behind the adults. Grandfather brought up the rear. The long line of wolves moved through an old burn where the silver trunks of the dead trees stood like silent ghosts guarding the white landscape. The wolves scrambled over some fallen trees and crawled under others.

The pack finally emerged from the woods into a huge meadow that overlooked the part of Lamar Valley where Soda Butte Creek flowed into the Lamar River. The 'K' Meadow, as it was called, looked like the letter 'k' if you happened to be a raven flying by. When Papa bedded in the meadow, the other wolves did likewise, including the tired pups. Alphie sat near Grandfather and looked out across the valley.

Chapter Four

A thin blanket of white covered the 'K' Meadow, but the valley below had no snow. The grass there was brown, and the aspen trees were gold. To the north were the *formidable* cliffs of Druid Peak with their stone spires, dark caves, and *horizontal* ledges. Below the cliffs was a long stone ledge called the Ledge Trail used by wolves for centuries to get to the Den Forest where both Alphie and Grandfather had been born.

East was Mount Norris, another mountain with cliffs hundreds of feet high. The meadows near the top were snow covered. Grandfather noticed Alphie studying Mount Norris and said, "Although we can't see them from here, there are bighorn sheep near the cliffs scraping the snow away to get at the grass. If a wolf, mountain lion, or bear comes along, the sheep climb out on narrow ledges on the cliffs for protection. Predators like us can't get to them there so it's a rare day that we get to feast on bighorn. Did you ever hear that saying 'Look before you leap'?"

Alphie said, "Papa said that when we were crossing the fast water of the creek."

"He was talking about reading the water," Grandfather said. "He wanted you to leap in way upstream from where you intended to land so that you would not get swept into the white water downstream.

"When I was a pup," Grandfather continued, "not much bigger than you, there was an old mountain lion who did not look before she leapt. For many years she made a good living on Mount Norris. But when she got old, she started taking chances. One evening the bighorns smelled her coming through the woods. They moved out of the meadow onto those ledges for safety. I happened to be on Puppy Hill near the bottom of the cliffs so I heard the shrill *yowl* of the cat when she leapt on a sheep that was near the edge of the cliff. The sheep lost its footing and fell with the cat holding onto its back. I didn't see them fall, but I heard their cries as they descended hundreds of feet. Then all was quiet. My grandfather, Old Gray, led our pack through a stand of trees to the bottom of the cliff where the sheep and the lion lay dead. Old Gray said that the lion should have looked before she leapt, should have considered the *consequences* of her actions."

"Grandfather," said Alphie, "what are consequences?"

"Good question," he said. "They're the results you get when you do something. If you eat something, you are no longer hungry. That is a good consequence. However, if you jump into fast, white water or jump over a cliff, the consequence you get will not be good. Before you do something you should ask yourself how it might hurt you or what trouble you will get into."

"You mean be careful," Alphie said.

"Yes, Alphie," Grandfather replied.

"I'm not too good at that," he yawned.

Grandfather whispered, "Get some sleep now. We'll head for the old rendezvous in the morning."

Alphie curled against Grandfather, closed his eyes slowly, and drifted into dreams.

Chapter Five

"Ahooooooohoooohooo." The distant howls were an unwelcome song on the morning wind. Grandfather was the first to hear it. He sat up and listened. "Ahoooooohoooohooo." The voices were coming from miles away across the valley near the Den Forest on the slope of Druid Peak. Mother Wolf, Papa, Cobalt and the others stood up and listened, all facing north. Grandfather nudged Alphie awake. He sat blinking, facing the wrong way.

"What is it, Grandfather?" asked the sleepy pup.

"Intruders," he said. "Turn around and listen. I hear at least four voices, maybe five."

Alphie heard the voices, as well, and instinctively knew that they meant trouble, just like the time Big Black of the Pelican Pack showed up on the Mirror Plateau. Alphie's pack had a large territory and spent a lot of time defending its borders. While the Lamar Pack had been at Opal Creek, the alphas, Cobalt, and others returned each week to Lamar Valley to scent mark their territorial boundaries as a warning to other packs to keep out. Even though the intruders knew this was Lamar Pack territory, they had ignored the warning signs.

As an additional warning to the intruders, Mother Wolf and Papa howled a reply. In wolf talk the alphas told the invading pack to get out of Lamar Valley. Then, as if the entire pack had been thinking the same thought, they ran like *warriors* across the 'K' Meadow to the Ridge Trail that led to the valley.

The pups had never run this fast before. They leapt over logs, scrambled over boulders, and dove under brush that blocked their path. Individual yelps could be heard as Slate bumped his head and Lupine scraped her shoulder. Alphie was the lead pup, but soon, even he could no longer see the adults that, with their long legs, shot down the hill. Grandfather stayed with the pups and guided them to the valley floor.

The pups followed Grandfather west across Chalcedony Creek to the Eastern Foothill, a long narrow mound not much higher than the back of a bison. The pups lined up on the hill with Grandfather at one end and Alphie at the other. From where they stood, the pups could see their pack charging toward the *interlopers* on the far side of the valley.

WOLF
42F
2006

2011

WOLF 21M
2006

Chapter Six

Neither the warning howls nor the sight of the approaching Lamar Pack frightened off the four trespassers. In fact, they had run from the Den Forest toward the advancing wolves. They crossed Soda Butte Creek in their rush to battle. The three grays and the black stopped on the bank of the Lamar River and bark-howled their challenge to the attacking Lamar wolves. With each bark, they would raise up on their hind legs to add emphasis to their claim to the valley. This territory was the best hunting ground in Yellowstone, and they intended to take it over. The courage of the intruders began to fade as the much larger pack advanced on their position. The four wolves saw that not only were they outnumbered, the Lamar wolves were big animals. The black wolf said, "Yikes! Let's get out of here!" All four tucked their tails, a sign of fear and submission, and ran for their lives just as the Lamar wolves splashed into the river.

From the safety of the Eastern Foothill, Alphie watched. He could see his parents pursue the intruders with the help of the other ten pack members. All the wolves were speeding north, then west at forty miles per hour. They flew by a dead tree where a half dozen ravens watched with interest. The pursued and pursuers crossed *21's Crossing,* where in the past many litters of pups had made their own Crossing to the rendezvous.

Alphie could see that beyond the confluence, the Lamar wolves overtook the intruding pack. There was much snarling, yelping, and biting as the invaders tumbled in the terrible wave of wolves that washed over them. Fur flew as the black and grays tried to make their escape down the valley. Satisfied that the unwanted guests had been taught a lesson, Mother Wolf and Papa bedded, as did most of the others. Cobalt and two yearlings continued escorting the trespassers past Rose Creek and out of the valley. The dark ravens tagged along.

Alphie was excited by all of the commotion. He moved to the Middle Foothill and then the Western Foothill to watch Cobalt continue the chase west. "Wow!" he said aloud to himself. His own heart was racing even though he had not chased anything.

It was at that moment that he heard a low growl behind him. Alphie looked over his shoulder. At the base of the hill crouching by an aspen trunk was a black wolf, a stranger, a fifth intruder. It had its teeth bared and was ready to leap on the wolf pup. Alphie turned and faced the trespasser. He returned the wolf's stare without tucking his tail. Alphie was much bigger now than when he was the lost pup of Lamar. He was still a pup, but a big pup.

Alphie bared his teeth and gave out his best growl. Then, inspired by the chase he had just witnessed, he took a step toward the black stranger. The black stood and stepped toward Alphie. The stranger was about to pounce on the pup when Grandfather stepped in front of him. He was smiling.

He said to the dark wolf, "Hello there, Yancey. It's been a long time."

Alphie tried to run past Grandfather to get at the black. Grandfather gently pushed the pup back behind him.

"Yes, Sweetie, it has been a while. I had heard a rumor that you were *rubbed out* last winter on Junction Butte. The Agates were around then."

Grandfather grinned. "Some rumors are not true. You know the Agate Pack likes to make up stories."

"I should have known better," Yancey said. "Is this runt yours?" She lifted a paw toward Alphie.

Alphie made an angry face and tried to get by Grandfather on the other side. Grandfather gently pushed him back.

"You're a long way from home, Yancey," Grandfather said. "Are those other four from the Garnet Hill Pack, too?"

"Yes," she said. "We heard another rumor that the Lamar Pack had moved out. This valley would make a nice addition to our territory."

Grandfather said, "As you can see, we're still here. You may want to take the Specimen Trail back west so that you don't run into Cobalt or the alphas. They're not in a good humor right now."

"Thanks for the advice," Yancey said. "I'll do that. The runt there will need more supervision if you expect him to make it to his first birthday. By the way, Sweetie, you still look good. Take care of yourself." Yancey turned and disappeared into the forest.

Grandfather turned to Alphie. "It takes a brave wolf to stand up to a stranger like that. I'm proud of you, but you might want to wait a year before you do it again. She could have rubbed you out. That would not be good. Remember what happened to the mountain lion."

Alphie spoke rapidly, "She was giving me the angry face, the bared teeth, the bad voice! I was going to show her that that is not nice, but then you stepped in!"

"Yes, yes, I know. You are a brave wolf," Grandfather said.

The two started walking back to the other pups when Alphie asked, "Grandfather, how did you know her name was Yancey?"

He said, "She's an old girlfriend of mine from way back. Before I became an alpha, I roamed a bit."

"Grandfather, what's a girlfriend?" Alphie asked.

"Well," he hesitated, "when you have a friend who is a girl and not your sister like Yarrow and Lupine, she's a girlfriend. It's a little more complicated, but that can wait until you're older."

Chapter Seven

Alphie remembered that he was back at the summer rendezvous; he was home. He ran to his flat rock and sniffed all around. He climbed onto the rock and howled his joy. The other pups answered and ran to join him. However, Alphie was already running toward the woods to investigate his secret cave. Half way there, the others overtook him and tried to tackle the excited pup. Instead, he jumped on them pinning each one in turn. Yarrow was so feisty that he couldn't hold her. She squirmed away and ran to the woods ahead of the rest.

All of the play helped them determine their own place in the puppy pack and would later help them find their position in the whole pack. Some would be *submissive*; some would be *dominant*. Alphie was proving to be a leader.

The others followed Alphie into the woods. Yarrow was already in the cave. They crowded in, pushing and shoving to make room. The cave had seemed larger when it was part of the summer rendezvous. Now that the pups had tripled in size, it was a tight squeeze. Alphie recounted for his brothers and sisters the stories of the angry bear, the terrible storm, and the attack of the mountain lion all of which had happened when he was left behind when the others moved to Opal Creek. He described how Grandfather had saved him and gave a detailed account of their long journey back to the family.

Alphie said, "When I grow up, I'm going to be just like Grandfather. I'll be brave like him and have lots of girlfriends."

"What are girlfriends?" Lupine asked.

"I don't know exactly, but they are important to have," Alphie said.

Several long howls could be heard coming from the foothills. All the pups turned toward the entrance of the cave.

Basalt said, "That's Mother calling us!"

They scrambled out and ran to the Middle Foothill where the pack had gathered for a family howl. Cobalt and the others had returned.

All joined the howl. "Ahooooohooooohooo," the pack sang their wild song. "Ooooohooohoo" the pups called out to the valley. They realized that this was the rally before the hunt. The wolves concluded the howl with play bowing, rubbing against each other, and much wagging of tails.

All of this joy made Grandfather feel younger, and he was pleased to tell the pups that they would not be left behind this time. They would go along on the hunt as observers. Grandfather explained, "You young ones will stay with me. We'll watch from a distance so you can learn how we hunt. It's a dangerous business, so pay close attention."

Chapter Eight

The Lamar Pack spread out across the south side of the valley with the alphas nearest the river, Cobalt and others in the sage covered flats, and Grandfather leading the pups along the edge of the forest. They headed downstream where Cobalt had seen a small herd of elk emerge from the woods near Amethyst Creek. The elk were headed for the river just north of Jasper Bench, a boulder strewn, grassy plateau where bison, antelope, and elk liked to graze.

The pack loped westward. The sun, just above Specimen Ridge, followed them. A dozen excited ravens squawked above, looking like a flock of shadows trailing the wolves. A *solitary* bald eagle watched from its perch on a standing, dead cottonwood near the riverbank. The base of the tree trunk had been chewed a great deal by beavers. A pair of sandhill cranes, almost ready to migrate south, gave their rattling call from a hillside meadow: karrrooo, karrrooo. A slight breeze caused the gold aspen leaves to quake.

Grandfather spoke to the pups as they paraded past the yellow trees. "Back during the dark days of the Disappearance when wolves did not live here, these trees were rubbed out by the *ungulates*, meaning elk, bison, antelope, and black-tail deer. Without a predator like us, the grazers had no reason to move from a spot until every green thing was eaten. New shoots, new saplings were devoured. The old trees died off. There were few new trees to replace the old ones. When wolves returned, that changed. We keep the herds alert and moving. More young aspen survive. The same is true for willows, cottonwoods, and grasses. They provide food and shelter for moose, beaver, and many birds. Why, even the river benefits by having the willow and cottonwood roots hold its banks together. Keeps it from getting wider, from becoming too shallow, too warm. Cutthroat trout need cold water. It's a nice balance. Also, for hundreds of thousands of years we have kept elk herds strong by taking out the weak ones. More balance."

The pups listened mostly, but play hunting distracted them. They stalked one another and jumped on each other practicing what they would do if they were grown up wolves.

The grown up wolves continued at a trot heading west. They passed through open grassy meadows, scattered cottonwood trees, and *eroded gullies*. As they approached Amethyst Creek, the alphas crossed the Lamar River and bedded on a knoll a few hundred yards from the elk. A pair of Barrow's goldeneyes exploded from the water and went whistling down stream. The other wolves found high ground as well. Most of them bedded; some sat, while Cobalt remained standing. All eyes were on the elk. Grandfather and the pups bedded on Jasper Bench where they had balcony seats to watch the drama that was about to unfold.

The elk herd consisted of a dozen cows, a few calves, and a bull with massive antlers. The cows were his *harem*, 'girlfriends' as Grandfather would say. Their white rumps had been visible when the wolves approached, but now, with *nostrils* full of wolf smell, the elk bunched together facing the predators that lay in the grass. They bumped each other as they tried to move closer together. Calves, much larger now than during the summer, were looking in all directions for the danger.

Several cows were still chewing grass as they looked at the wolves. One large cow stamped her hooves and blew air through her nose as a warning to the wolves. She took several steps forward and stamped her hooves again. The bull, a healthy seven hundred pound animal, put his head back and bugled loudly. His long squeal pierced the length of the valley like a siren.

Mother Wolf and Papa jumped to their feet, raced down the slope, and splashed into the icy river. The current carried them downstream a little way so that when they emerged from the water they were close to the elk. Cobalt led the attack from the east. The elk bolted west along the river. The alphas cut off their retreat and turned the herd back toward the rest of the pack.

The elk held their heads high as they ran, trying to show that they were too healthy for the wolves to bother *pursuing*. Grandfather explained to the pups, "We chase a herd to see if any of the animals are sick, injured, or weak from age. The weaker elk are easier to take down and safer for us. A healthy elk can kill a wolf with its hooves or antlers. We have lost a dozen of our brothers and sisters to elk. A good hunter knows this is dangerous work, so he chooses his prey carefully."

"He?" Yarrow said. "What about me?"

"Or she," Grandfather corrected himself.

The pups could hear the desperate cries of the calves. The thundering hooves of the elk shook the ground. The sound went through the pups like an electric current. Alphie and the other pups, excited by the chase, sat up. Alphie stood and was about to run down the high slope to join the chase when he remembered the story of the mountain lion. 'Look before you leap,' he heard Grandfather's voice in his head. He knew that even though he felt the same rushing excitement of the adults, he was still a pup and had no hunting skills. His experience was with ground squirrels and bugs, not five hundred pound elk. Alphie sat and whined.

Grandfather said, "You just made a good decision. I know what's going on in your head and heart, but, for now, we just watch and learn. Your turn will come soon." As he spoke, Yarrow stood up and seemed to be ready to spring down the hill.

The elk were twenty yards ahead of the wolves, each of which was running like a gust of wind toward the river. The river exploded like erupting *geysers* as the bull, cows, and calves plunged into a deep hole near the bend. The water was almost chest deep. Yarrow whined.

Grandfather said to the pups, "Elk know we don't like to attack in water. They're safe for now."

The sky was silver-blue. The moving water was the color of sky. The liquid sky pulled at the elk with its current.

The wolves bedded on both banks of the river. They had the elk surrounded so there was no hurry. They breathed heavily from the hard chase. Plumes of breath made visible by the cold air hung above the wolves for a moment before mingling with the elks' breath, both of which blended with the river's breath, steam rising in ghostly forms above the water.

Downstream in a stretch of whitewater, a dipper, a small, gray bird, continued diving into the fast, frigid water for bugs. It was unaware of the life and death struggle occurring nearby. Upstream in a calm pool, a wedge of ripples made by an otter moved away from the disturbance.

Yarrow looked at Alphie, shifted her feet, and whined again. She looked back at the elk just as the big cow climbed out of the water where the bank was low and sprinted toward Jasper Bench.

Chapter Nine

Mother Wolf, Papa, and Cobalt knew that the escaping cow was too healthy, too fast for them. They had their sights set on an old cow that had stumbled several times before taking *refuge* in the stream. She would be an easier target.

As the big cow rushed below Grandfather and the pups, just a hundred yards away, Alphie's little sister bolted down the steep slope hoping to catch the escaping animal.

Grandfather called out, "No, Yarrow! Come back! She's too big for you!"

Yarrow did not hear or chose not to listen. She held her dark gray tail out straight. The gray fur of her back and the silver fur along her sides rippled as she ran. As she darted down the slope, sometimes she jumped in order to see over tall clumps of sage.

The bald eagle in the dead tree watched the drama. Ravens bumped and slapped each other with their wings as they took flight to follow the action up the valley.

Alphie could see that his sister was in danger. He raced down the hill, a black streak with a raised tail. Grandfather cried out again, "No, Alphie! Come back! It's too dangerous! Come back!"

Grandfather's words went unanswered. Then he felt more furry bodies brush by him. Obsidian, Basalt, Lupine, and Slate charged down the hill following their brother.

"Foolish puppies," Grandfather muttered to himself. "Someone's going to get hurt or killed. I'm just too old for this." With a great sigh Grandfather loped down the hill to help as best he could.

Meanwhile, in the river, the bull elk, his cows, and the calves began to panic. They saw more wolves pouring off the hill; they saw the big cow sprinting away. The calves pressed against their mothers that bellowed and splashed wildly. Two more cows found the low riverbank and fled like the wind to the east. The wolves stood up *simultaneously*. Cobalt could see that the pups were nearing the base of the slope. He curled his lip and snarled his displeasure with the fact that they were interrupting the hunt. The remaining elk charged out of the waterhole leaving a wet trail as they ran for their lives.

As the disorganized parade of elk, wolf pups, and adult wolves moved toward Amethyst Creek, the small bison herd grazing there watched but did not move. The bison were like scattered boulders, and, because of their massive size and curved horns, they had little to fear from wolves.

A pronghorn antelope was watching from the other side of the river. He was a handsome buck with a rusty brown back and face with white on his sides, belly, and chin. Although wolves often chased antelope, the antelope was faster. If a wolf ran forty miles per hour, four times faster than a human, an antelope could run sixty miles per hour. The wolf evolved with the slower elk, while the antelope evolved over hundreds of thousands of years with the cheetah. In fact, this antelope looked more like an animal that might be seen on the African plains rather than here in Yellowstone. The buck sensed that the wolves were not after him, so he just watched the drama and chewed clumps of grass.

Calves bleated, cows shrieked, and the bull bugled as they broke through the line of wolves. Mother Wolf and Papa caught up with the rest of the pack, and the chase was on. Cobalt was out in front. They did not notice that one of the cows stayed behind in the river. It was the old one. Away from the confusion of the chase, she slowly waded downstream heading for the safety of the trees in Lamar Canyon.

The wolves continued to push the herd trying to locate the old elk. Then the bull stopped running. He turned, faced the wolves, and lowered his antlers determined to make a stand, to defend his harem, his girls. He pawed the ground with a hoof as the line of wolves approached. The bull was startled when the wolves ran right past him.

Chapter Ten

The bull elk whirled around and chased after the wolves that were chasing the cows that appeared to be chasing Grandfather who was trying to catch up with the pups that were chasing the big cow elk. A cloud of brown dust rose and settled on the sagebrush.

Alphie was not after the elk; he wanted to stop Yarrow before she got hurt. Of course, Yarrow could not run as fast as the elk. The only way she could catch it would be if it stopped, which is exactly what the big cow did.

Also, several other cows broke away from the group, and a few yearling wolves trailed after them. Grandfather had caught up with the four pups following Alphie. The large group of elk cows had overtaken the pups, and now Grandfather. Grandfather growled at the cows and barked at the pups to get out of the way, go back to the hill. But Lupine, Obsidian, Basalt, and Slate were yipping and yapping, having a great time on their first hunt and unaware of the danger that surrounded them.

Mother Wolf, Papa, and Cobalt raced ahead of the rest of the Lamar Pack. They were no longer hunting, but instead, trying to save the pups. They knew that death hung on the elks' hooves. A sudden kick, a misstep could be the end of a pup or, for that matter, an adult wolf. The three large wolves leapt at the cows trying to frighten them away from the small wolves running among them.

The elks' panic doubled, and they scattered in all directions. Some circled back to the bull. Three headed for the hills. The remainder ran over the pups. A sharp squeal was heard. Obsidian went down. Grandfather hurled himself against the closest cow and bit at her shoulder. She swung left pushing the other cows away from the pups. The cows headed north toward the safety of the river.

Grandfather, Papa, and Cobalt pinned the three pups to the ground with opened jaws and growled for them to stay put.

"What a mess you all have made of this hunt!" said Cobalt.

Papa said, "You could have been killed!"

"I'm too old for this," whispered Grandfather who was panting heavily.

Mother Wolf ran to Obsidian who was on his side near a driftwood log. She nudged him with her nose. He squealed softly. She nudged him again, and he sat up. Mother Wolf rubbed his face with hers. He held his right paw off the ground. She licked at some blood on the injured paw. Obsidian stood and moved toward the other pups, but he was limping badly.

When Mother Wolf turned to follow him, she saw the big cow elk way up the valley charge Yarrow. The cow ran straight for the small wolf. Yarrow froze.

Alphie called to her, "Run, little sister! Run!"

Just as the cow was about to kick out with her front hooves, Yarrow regained her courage and dashed left toward the river. The cow made a sharp turn and pursued the young wolf. Yarrow zigzagged through the sage. The cow did the same, kicking or stomping each time she got close to the wolf pup. A coyote popped out from behind a rock, saw the chase, and made a hasty retreat.

Alphie ran straight toward the river. The crescent moon on his chest rose and fell as he jumped over sagebrush and badger holes. He called out to Yarrow once again, "Cross the river! That will slow her down!"

Yarrow and the cow reached the riverbank at the same time. The cow rose up on her hind feet in an attempt to stomp the frightened wolf. At that moment Alphie leapt at the cow clamping his teeth like a trap on her foreleg. So startled was she that she lost her balance and fell on her side. Alphie did not let go.

Yarrow splashed into the silver water and swam to safety on the other side. She shook herself off and turned back to see if Alphie was okay. He wasn't.

The cow tried to kick Alphie with her back legs; tried to bite him; tried to shake him loose. He would not let go. She was able to get to her feet and jump off the bank into the river. The small black wolf was still holding on when she hit the water. However, the cow was able to hold Alphie under the water until he let go. He surfaced a few feet downstream gasping and spitting. The cow scrambled out of the river and disappeared to the north.

At that point Grandfather plunged into the river and let the current hold Alphie against his old body as he swam to the shallows. Alphie parallel walked with Grandfather, meaning he leaned against him as they moved onto a pebble beach. Alphie collapsed on the stones. Grandfather and Yarrow licked his face, his ears, and his legs. Alphie's chest heaved as if he couldn't get enough air.

The rest of the Lamar Pack crossed the river and circled the fallen pup. Obsidian limped into the circle and laid down by Alphie.

Mother Wolf whispered softly to her son, "You're the hero of this day, Alphie. And there will be more days like this one once you rest."

Lupine and Yarrow lay against Alphie to keep him warm. Basalt and Slate did likewise. The other wolves bedded where they were. Quiet settled over the scene except for the whispering cottonwoods and the murmur of the Lamar River. The sun slid along Specimen Ridge to the west and turned the sky blood red.

Yarrow woke up when she felt a gentle kick, then a push. "Slate, cut that out," she whispered.

Slate whispered back, "I didn't do anything."

Yarrow felt another kick. "Basalt, is that you?" she asked.

"Not me," he said.

Then she felt a big push from four paws as Alphie rolled over on his back and then stood up as the other pups rose to their feet.

"Alphie!" Yarrow cried.

Alphie began to run in tight circles around his brothers and sisters. He would stop suddenly, play bow, then run in the opposite direction. They all began to chase him calling "Alphie! Alphie!" They jumped on and over the adults rousing them from their drowsy dreams.

Cobalt leapt up and trapped Alphie with his great paws. All the pups stopped their celebration. They knew Cobalt to be a serious wolf, and they feared him.

With Mother Wolf and Papa listening, Cobalt spoke to the pups. "It's a poor day when pups interfere with a hunt. Because of you pups, none of us will eat today. Fall is a hard time for us. The calves are too big, the bulls and cows are in their prime, too healthy, too fast. You need to think about that. We survive by working together. As you grow, you'll find this to be true.

"However, what I saw today was more important than food. Alphie's bravery saved Yarrow. It is a good thing to witness courage in one so young. I am proud to be part of a pack that has such a fearless wolf as one of its members."

Alphie looked at Grandfather. He was smiling.

Mother Wolf and Papa began to howl. "Aahoooooohooooohooo!" they sang. The others joined. Woven among the twelve adult voices were the high-pitched cries of the pups. "Oooohoohoo!" They howled a centuries' old tribute to the elk which echoed in the elks' ears as they retreated west. The wolves howled long life to the family. They howled their delight that Alphie was not injured. They sang the honor song for Alphie's bravery, and they howled the pack's joy at returning to their wild home, the Lamar Valley.

Part 3
Winter

Alphie's Winter Adventure

OTTER ON ICE
Big wolf @ Slough
Bison calf head on carcass
Hellroaring Pack
Raven
Bedded Black Male
Snoozing Coyote In Lamar
Bald Eagle
Raven In Flight
Bison Calf
Cow Bison

Chapter One

The icy air around Garnett Peak sparkled with fairy dust crystals, floating in the silver light of sunrise. At thirty below zero, only two things moved across the snow fields east of Elk Creek: a shadowy raven and Alphie, the black wolf pup with a crescent moon on his chest. The raven flapped from snowdrift to snowdrift, landed, and, with his dark eyes, watched the wolf pass. The animal's steady *gait* stirred up snow that lay like sugar on the crust below. Alphie's winter coat was thick and plush, perfect protection against the subzero temperatures. The raven fluffed his feathers to keep warm. As he watched the wolf, he could hear the rhythmic, soft drumming of those immense paws and the panting breaths, which plumed above Alphie as he moved.

Here and there the white blanket was marked with the top of a sage bush poking through the snow, or a tall lodgepole pine standing alone casting a long shadow, or the pale scar of a small stream moving under snow toward Elk Creek. Alphie crossed several trails left by bison that had pushed snow aside with their huge heads in order to get at the meager grass below. The imprint in snow of a pair of wings told the story of how a vole or shrew had met his end, how the owl had moved through the white darkness on silent wings and snatched the life away that gave him life.

The raven hoped that the wolf was hunting and, if successful, might leave a few scraps on the snow to see him through the day.

Occasionally the bird would squawk encouragement and do a little hopping, flapping dance. But Alphie was not out for a hunt on this February day. He was headed for home, for the Lamar Valley.

Alphie stopped on a ridge overlooking the Yellowstone River fifty feet below. The river exhaled its steamy breath, scenting the cold air with the odor of sulfur. Just downstream from the open water of the rapids was an ice bridge, the same one he had crossed several days before. Just downstream from the bridge, the Lamar River joined the Yellowstone.

Alphie was about to drop down to the river when he heard a wolf howl. A second voice joined the first. He looked back over the wide expanse of the snowy field he had just crossed. There, at the far edge of the field on a snow covered bluff, stood three wolves, two blacks and a gray. Alphie knew that he was in Garnett Peak Pack territory and that, most likely, the three wolves were members of that pack. He knew that he would have to run like the wind to escape these wolves, and did so when he saw the wolves rush off the bluff and sprint toward him with their tails held high. Among wolves it is well known that if they trespass on another pack's territory, they are risking their lives.

Alphie plunged down the snowy slope to the ice bridge, crossed it in just a few strides, and bounded up the east slope. Although still a pup at ten months old, he was as big as some adults in his pack. His long, powerful legs had served him well in both chasing and retreating. He was now in retreat.

Alphie hesitated on the far side to look back, but he was too low to see the meadow. The wolf pup took deep breaths as his chest heaved. He turned east and climbed the steep side of Junction Butte, not stopping until he reached the summit four hundred feet above the river. Looking back from this high vantage point, Alphie could see the three wolves, much closer now, just descending to the river. Alphie whirled around and dashed across the windswept plateau of the butte. The young wolf practically slid down the eastern slope, plowing through powdery snowdrifts, the white dust rising behind him in a cloud. He heard another howl coming from his pursuers. They were already on top of the butte. Alphie realized that they were gaining on him and that he would have to run faster in order to make his escape.

Like all wolves, Alphie was designed for winter travel. His narrow, wedge shaped chest helped him to plow through deep snow. His large paws were like snowshoes. His *stamina* would allow him to run great distances. While the young pup had all of these advantages, so did the three wolves skidding down the slope of the butte, the same wolves whose pounding paws Alphie could hear on the frozen crust behind him.

A very puppy thought came to Alphie, causing him to stop and turn toward the oncoming wolves. Maybe they just want to play, he thought. But their growls convinced him that that was not their intention. He turned and ran for all he was worth.

Alphie was a black streak racing across the boulder-strewn valley just south of the Lamar River. Each of the bison-sized boulders had been rolled here from distant mountains thousands of years ago by the glacier that had sculpted this valley. Some boulders, called 'nursery rocks', had a single lodgepole growing next to them. Alphie wove his way through the boulders heading for the Peregrine Hills, low, rocky knolls that appeared half way up the valley. If only he could make it there, the Garnett wolves might leave him alone.

Chapter Two

Suddenly a gray wolf was running right next to Alphie matching him stride for stride. The wolf's silver winter coat was just a shade darker than the snow swirling around him. His muzzle was white. Alphie's heart clenched. Then he cried out, "Grandfather! It's you! Where did you come from?"

The old wolf smiled. "I was watching you from Specimen Ridge, up high by the *Petrified Forest*. Your friends are from the Garnett Pack. We chased them out of the Lamar Valley last fall, remember?"

"Yes, I do, and they're not my friends," gasped Alphie. "Can we talk about this later? They're gaining on us!"

"Follow me," Grandfather said. "I know a short cut."

The pair turned south at the Peregrine Hills and crossed the valley to the base of Specimen Ridge. The two wolves had run full speed through a small herd of twenty bison stirring them into a frenzy, which caused them to stampede through deep snow, bellowing and bumping each other. Snow exploded in every direction. The bison ran north away from Alphie and Grandfather and directly toward the three Garnett wolves.

Grandfather shouted, "That ought to keep those wolves busy for a while. If you aren't faster than they are, it helps to be a little smarter."

Alphie grinned. He loved how Grandfather could turn trouble into play, and how he always showed up at just the right moment. He felt safer when Grandfather was around, and he hoped the old wolf would always be there to teach him how to survive and how to laugh.

"Where are we headed?" Alphie asked.

"You'll see," said the old wolf.

Grandfather led the young wolf into heavy timber where lodgepole pines grew so thick snow barely covered the ground. They stopped near a large hole dug in the slope of the hill. Brown earth, *excavated* from the den years ago, formed a compact mound at the entrance. A nearby aspen tree had four long grooves on either side. Alphie remembered Grandfather had explained once before that such marks were made by the claws of a grizzly bear, an animal that, at this time of year, was asleep somewhere in a den under the snow.

Alphie asked, "What's this place?"

"This is a special place for me," the old wolf said. "This is Old Mother's den. She was one of the first wolves to come back here after the Disappearance. She only had one litter of pups in this den, but one pup in that litter was my great grandfather. Of the eight pups she had, he and four others became alphas of their own packs. If Old Mother hadn't had that litter, I wouldn't be here; you wouldn't be here. When a young wolf dies, all the generations that would have followed die with her or him. Fortunately for you and me, Old Mother lived a long life and had many litters. You could say that there is a little bit of her in most of the wolves along the Yellowstone."

"Grandfather?" Alphie asked.

"What?" said Grandfather.

"Shouldn't we be going?'

"Oh, yes. I forgot we're being chased. Let's go this way."

Grandfather, with Alphie trailing behind, trotted east through thick woods and across open snowfields, the treeless paths of old avalanches. They passed some standing dead trees whose trunks were bleached to a silvery gray by the sun, the same gray as Grandfather's coat. He and the black pup gradually moved high on Specimen Ridge passing just down slope from the thick stone pillars of Petrified Forest, each tree standing like a rock guardian watching over the white valley.

They continued across the upper run of Crystal Creek moving on to the treeless Divide Ridge, which separated the creek from the Lamar Valley, their home territory. Grandfather stopped at this invisible boundary and looked back. Alphie did the same. Huge snow cliffs hung along the steep upper slopes of Specimen Ridge. Tall lodgepole pines were covered with heavy snow, ivory pillars, with their branches weighed down beneath the white powder. The valley was a linen sheet across which many tracks intersected. To save energy in winter, elk and bison often walked in single file creating well-worn trails across the white landscape.

Grandfather sat. So did Alphie. The old wolf settled down into the snow and said, “I guess our escort got lost.”

Alphie laid down in the snow and replied, “The angry bison must have made those wolves forget about us. I can just picture the bison chasing the wolves every which way.”

Grandfather said, “There is an old story about three wild horses walking a trail. The first horse steps on a bee’s nest in the ground. By the time the angry bees got organized enough to attack, the second horse had already gone by. It was the third horse that the bees went after stinging him so that he went bucking off into the woods. We just stirred up bigger bees, and the Garnett wolves got all the attention.”

Alphie laughed and laughed. In his imagination he was seeing winged bison chasing wolves. He thought he could even hear yelps from the wolves each time one got stung.

The wind along the Divide Ridge was just enough to create a soft hum, a natural song that worked its magic on the tired pair who soon closed their eyes and slept. The cold ball of the silvery sun crept ever so slowly across the blue sky like an escaped balloon until it balanced on the plateau of Junction Butte to the west. A few clouds had drifted in from the west. Their thick centers were dark gray, but the edges of the clouds were crimson, a cranberry red with *fairyslipper* pink shafts of light streaking the sky like the spokes of a wheel. The red light stained the snow, the trees, and the sleeping wolves the color of fire

Chapter Three

Grandfather was the first to stir. He yawned, stretched, rolled onto his back, and wriggled in the snow with his legs in the air. The temperature of the frigid air had dropped to forty below. When he finally opened his eyes, he realized that it was dark. He was staring up at a sky filled with millions of stars, each one appearing like a hole in the black blanket of the sky through which silver light leaked.

Grandfather sat up and saw a white glow at the far end of Lamar Valley. It was the snow moon rising. He remembered his own grandfather had called it 'wolf moon', and an uncle who was a poor hunter called the February moon 'hunger moon'. Good names all, he thought. Grandfather felt Alphie stretch against him. The young wolf sat up and blinked. He's getting so big, Grandfather thought. Both sat silently for a long while watching the immense moon rise above Thunderer Mountain spreading its pale light over the valley revealing the broad silver scar in the snow that was the Lamar River. Where there was open water, the river's breath rose into the moonlight.

Grandfather finally broke the silence. "I meant to ask you, Alphie, what you were doing in Garnett Pack territory? What were you thinking going so far away from the family?"

"Sorry, Grandfather," Alphie replied. "A few days ago I followed Cobalt all the way to a place he called Blacktail Plateau. I thought he was going to teach me more about hunting, but that wasn't his reason for crossing the Garnett Pack territory. He was looking for a girlfriend!

"Once we were there, he howled and howled. I did, too. I thought it was a way to call the elk to us. But it wasn't. We heard howls answering from Lava Creek. Soon enough, two gray females showed up. They started jumping on Cobalt and laughing and playing. But when I joined in on the fun, Cobalt pinned me on my back and growled for me to get lost, to go home. That's how I ended up crossing Garnett Peak alone."

Alphie could see in the moonlight that Grandfather was smiling. Finally, the old wolf said, "Cobalt shouldn't have let you tag along. You're only ten months old; still a pup. A big pup, it's true, but still a pup. Often when we wolves turn about two, we leave the pack to find a mate. Cobalt has waited twice that long. He'll be four this spring. Come to think of it, he did go off last winter, but he came home quickly, a little beat up. Some male wolves that didn't like him hanging around answered his *serenade*. From what you say, it sounds like he's having better luck this time. Cobalt might start his own pack, or he may come back home. We'll have to wait and see. Meanwhile, I want you to promise to stay near the family; don't leave the valley. You promise?"

"Yes, Grandfather," Alphie said. "It's too scary out there. Thank you for watching out for me."

"You're welcome," Grandfather whispered. "Now let's go find Mother Wolf and Papa!"

After scent marking along the Divide Ridge, Grandfather and Alphie bolted down the long descending trail to the Lamar River. They trotted between the stream and the steep, treed slope above which was Jasper Bench, a flat snowfield dotted with boulders capped with snow. Alphie tackled Grandfather several times rolling him in the snow. They took turns placing paws on each other's backs followed by play bowing and romping in circles. Near Amethyst Creek, Alphie ran ahead and hid behind a fallen log near the frozen waterfall. The gurgling water under the ice sounded like laughter. Alphie *ambushed* Grandfather when he trotted by, and Grandfather pretended to be surprised. They both rolled in the snow before continuing east along the river, a pair of shadows drifting across a sea of snow, their white wake sparkling in the moon's light. The wolf moon hung above Specimen Ridge like a white flower encircled by a milky halo, a sign of change in the weather, a storm on its way.

Grandfather and Alphie appeared to be wading through jewels as the snow glistened in the moon's light. They passed through a long row of leafless cottonwood trees. Ahead lay the low foothills and the rendezvous site of the Lamar Pack. Grandfather knew that even in moonlight, the pack might think that they are strangers, so he stopped and howled to announce their arrival. "Ahooohooohoooooooo," he sang. Alphie, now an older pup, had an older pup's voice, lower like that of an adult. He howled, too. "Ahooohooohoooooooo!" Several voices answered from the foothills. Alphie recognized Mother Wolf's voice and knew that he was finally home.

Mother Wolf and a gray yearling trotted out to meet Alphie and Grandfather. The four wolves wagged tails, rubbed against each other, licked faces, and jumped on one another in greeting. Mother Wolf stepped back and looked at Alphie. "Where have you been?" she asked.

"With Cobalt on the Blacktail Plateau," he answered. "Cobalt said I could go with him, but then he sent me home alone."

"That Romeo should not have taken you on his adventures. You're too young," she said. "Did you have any trouble?"

"A little, but Grandfather took care of it," he said looking at the ground.

"You remember, Grandfather, that last year Cobalt disappeared for a few weeks. He came back a little roughed up. Maybe he'll come back again. He's a good hunter and could teach you young ones how to read an elk."

Alphie looked puzzled. "Read an elk?" he said.

Mother Wolf explained, "If you try to take down a healthy elk, it could kill you. We have to look for the weakest animals, ones that are sick, injured or *malnourished*, starving. In order to find the weak one, we chase the herd long enough to see which one is slow or which one stumbles. As a wolf, you have to know what to look for, what the signs are. Cobalt could teach you how to read those signs. We have had some wolves in this pack that were not good readers. They are no longer with us."

Grandfather said, "If Cobalt doesn't return, I can teach you to read. Midnight is a good hunter. He's three already, and I'm sure he'll help, too."

"Papa and I will help, as well," said Mother Wolf.

Alphie said, "I want to be the best reader in the pack! Hey, where is everyone?"

"Oh, they're all asleep," said Mother Wolf. "We just returned from a hunt, and everyone is worn out."

"Good! I'm starving!" said Alphie.

Mother said, "Unfortunately the hunt was not successful. We'll have to try again after everyone has rested. Eating will have to wait."

Grandfather bedded on the middle foothill near Papa and Mother Wolf. Alphie found the other pups behind the western foothill. He turned three times in a tight circle and bedded. The rest of the pack was spread out among the foothills, each curled against the bitter cold, and each muzzle covered with a paw. On the moon lit snow, the dark shapes of the wolves appeared like rocks scattered there thousands of years ago by a glacier. The ancient moon above, with its halo, crossed the winter sky leaving in its wake a stream of stars that sparkled like crystals on a chandelier.

Chapter Four

In the morning Lupine and Yarrow, Alphie's sisters, woke Alphie by jumping on him and licking his face.

"Get up, Sleepy!" Lupine cried.

"Where have you been?" asked Yarrow.

Alphie sprang to his feet but was knocked over and pinned by his sisters. At almost seventy pounds each, they could hold down their big brother. Before Alphie could answer the question, his three brothers were all over him. For several minutes there was a large wolf pup pile accompanied by many yips and yaps. When all the pups regained their footing, Alphie took off across the foothills leaping over sleeping adults. The other pups did the same. Obsidian slid on the snow and crashed into Papa who jumped up and snarled at the pup. Obsidian immediately rolled over on his back in a sign of submission and whined his apologies to his father. Papa licked snow off Obsidian's face. Basalt and Slate, Alphie's other brothers, leapt on Papa rolling him in the snow. Then they scrambled away with Papa in pursuit.

All of the commotion woke the rest of the pack. They were pleased to see Alphie and showed it by chasing him around the foothills. Even Mother Wolf and Grandfather joined the other ten adults and five pups trying to capture Alphie. Snow rose up from all the running wolves, and after all the slipping and sliding, the whole pack looked like snow wolves, white from head to paw.

Finally, they pinned Alphie and smothered him with wolf kisses and rubs. The family bonds strengthened. They were all as one. In this wild place, the strong family bond was one more layer of protection that contributed to the survival of each of the pack members.

Papa was the first to howl. "Ahoohoooohoooo!" he sang. Before his song was swallowed by the immense silence of the valley, all the others began to howl as well. The long bass notes of this wild chorus carried up and down the valley and echoed off the snow cliffs of Specimen Ridge and Druid Peak. The ravens in the pines heard the call. A herd of bison heard the song. A line of elk moving through the forest picked up their pace just in case the wolves were talking about them.

As it happened, the wolves noticed the faint smell of elk. The one wolf missing from the pack, Cobalt, usually led the hunt, but he was away. Midnight, a three year old, one hundred twenty pound black wolf, took his place. As Midnight headed south, the rest of the pack lined up behind him. The pups, now almost as big as the adults, were old enough to go hunting with them. Mother Wolf and Grandfather reminded the pups to watch how the older wolves chased the elk herd to find the weakest animal to take down.

"You must learn to read the elk," Mother Wolf reminded them. "Your reading skill may save your life!"

Grandfather whispered to Alphie, "Stay focused. No fooling around."

"Yes, Grandfather," he sighed. Lupine and Yarrow giggled.

The wolves moved along the edge of the forest to Chalcedony Creek, which trickled off Specimen Ridge under deep snow. Midnight led the train of wolves through an old burn of standing dead lodgepoles and up a trail to 'K' Meadow, on the ridge overlooking the valley. Midnight sniffed some elk tracks, first following them up to the edge of the high woods, then backtracking downhill along No Name Creek to the Lamar River. A wolf's sense of smell is so keen that it can tell from the scent of a set of tracks which way the animal is traveling.

The rest of the Lamar Pack followed. The pups tried to stay focused but occasionally nipped at one another's wagging tail or pushed each other into snowdrifts. They always acted surprised when scolded by Mother Wolf.

Even though the sun was bright and the landscape was ablaze with light, the temperature was near twenty below. Dark clouds to the west, however, fulfilled the promise of what the ring around the moon had foretold: a storm was on its way. Soon it would warm up enough to snow.

Chapter Five

The elk tracks led into a long stand of cottonwood trees through which the Lamar River ran. The leafless branches and thick, dark tree trunks stood in stark contrast to the white snow. Midnight followed the tracks across a snow bridge into thick willows, which grew among the cottonwoods. The pack drew closer to Midnight, and all were sniffing the icy air. They were no longer smelling tracks. The scent of elk was everywhere.

Several dozen cow elk, and a few young bulls were huddled up in the dense cover of the willows. They bumped each other as they gathered closer together. The steaming breath of the elk rose above the reddish-brown willow stems. Hooves shuffled in the snow as the scent of wolf filled their nostrils. Each elk was intently watching through the willows as the dark wolf forms paced back and forth. The river gurgled, and ice clinked along its bank, sounds that mixed with the panting of the wolves and the nervous whispers among the elk.

Alphie moved through the pack to stand next to Midnight. The dark wolf growled at him. "Don't get in the way, kid!" he warned. "Just watch and learn."

Alphie nodded.

Midnight turned and rushed into the thick willows. The stems whipped wildly showering the wolf with snow. The elk exploded from their hiding place, climbed frantically up the bank of the old riverbed, and thundered through the snow across the open sage flats toward

Mount Norris. The elk herd moved as one the way a flock of birds will move as if controlled by a single mind. Together they zigged or zagged, depending on where their pursuers were. The wolves, pups included, spread out behind the fleeing elk, gradually closing the gap between predator and prey. In the air above the drama, a dozen wildly flapping ravens cheered the wolves on in hopes that lunch would be served after the final act.

Alphie ran just behind Midnight and watched his every move. Grandfather's words repeated themselves in the pup's mind: 'The chase helps us determine the health of the elk. They will run with their heads held high trying to tell us that they are too healthy for us to pursue. We have to decide if that's true.'

To Alphie, all of the elk appeared to be in good shape. As the pack closed in on the elk, the herd divided into two groups. Half headed up Soda Butte Creek; half crossed the lap of Mount Norris. Obsidian, Alphie's dark gray brother, was the only wolf that followed the animals running east along Soda Butte Creek. The rest of the wolves had already determined that those elk were telling the truth and were too strong to bring down.

Alphie ran stride for stride just behind Midnight. The pup watched the big male as he tested individual cows and one of the young bulls. Alphie knew that Midnight was reading them, looking for a misstep, a lack of stamina, breathing more labored than the others, or an irregular stride or limp. All were signs of possible weakness. Alphie noticed that even as Midnight was running full speed across the snow, he was sniffing the air for fear, perhaps, or disease, or injury, any one of which could mean an easy meal. Of course, taking down an animal five times your size was rarely easy.

Earlier hunts that Alphie had participated in had been trial and error on his part, mostly error. He hadn't paid attention to the whole reading thing; he hadn't looked for signs of weakness, signs that would tell him that an elk was *vulnerable*. He didn't know then that a healthy elk could kill a wolf. Instead he felt he knew what to do and that his strength and speed were enough. In fact, a few weeks earlier Grandfather had watched Alphie chase a big bull elk for five miles down the valley, jumping in and out of the river. Finally, the elk became angry, stopped, and faced the young wolf, its breath steaming like smoke. The bull lowered his head so that all Alphie could see were a dozen antler tines, sharp as spearheads, pointing at him. The elk charged. Alphie drew in his breath in surprise and ran back toward the rendezvous site with his tail tucked and his ears flattened, the pursuer being pursued.

Back then, Grandfather just shook his head and smiled at the wet pup. He did not interfere. He said to Alphie, "I think that bull taught you a valuable lesson. Elk and wolf have been teaching each other for thousands of years. Soon you will learn even more from your own kind."

Now was that time. Alphie was careful not to get in Midnight's way, but he did do his best to imitate everything the black wolf did. At the very moment that Midnight chose which elk to take down, Alphie knew which one it was and why. The old cow's rapid breath was raspy; her strides were shorter than the others, her eyes were wild, her tongue hung loose, she bleated her fear, and she held her head low as if weary of hurting, weary of hunger, weary of winter.

Once Midnight caught up with the old cow, he did not hesitate; he did not think 'Is this right or wrong' because he knew this was the way of all wild things. The trout eats the fly; the osprey eats the trout. The shrew eats the beetle; the owl eats the shrew. It's nature's way; it's Midnight's way.

DEAD BULL
JUNCTION BUTTE
FROM PHOTO
SAME SKULL FROM PHOTO

5/16/02 Druid wolves in Lamar Valley
- Feeding on buffalo carcass

529
526
380
All have
bars on chest
more white on face though
629F
w/FULL BELLY
gray pup - smaller

Chapter Six

Hours later when the pack had finished eating, Obsidian showed up. He was wet, cold, and hungry. All of the adults were too full of meat and too sleepy to even greet the returning pup. A few heads rose for a look, and then went down again. Alphie, Basalt, and Slate were playing a game of tag with their sisters. Lupine and Yarrow tried to get Obsidian to join the chase, but he just wanted to eat and sleep, which is exactly what he did.

As the tired pup lay curled in a ball with one paw over his muzzle, snowflakes landed on his damp fur. The white crystals fell on all the sleeping wolves. Their thick fur kept the flakes from melting. Alphie and the others, playing their running games, shed the white powder as it fell. Soon the afternoon light dimmed, and, in the rising temperature, the snowflakes became larger and more numerous, falling like down feathers from a snow goose. All the sleeping wolves became white lumps under the snow, a collection of wolf sculptures.

Alphie's brothers and sisters chased him farther and farther up the Lamar River, trying to capture the prize stick he was carrying. Their playful barks and squeals grew fainter as they receded up the white valley. The cloud cover thickened and grew *ominously* dark. The snowfall doubled in intensity, whiting out Druid Peak, Mount Norris, and Specimen Ridge. As the playful pups moved even farther south up the valley, the lower part of the river *vanished* behind them.

Yarrow climbed a snowy slope and slid down face first on her belly. Alphie dropped his stick, ran up the slope, and slid down half backwards and half sideways. The other three pups did the same, plowing headfirst or tail first down the white slide. All were laughing and covered with snow.

The laughing stopped when Slate said, "Hey, there's a coyote!"

The coyote was half the size of the pups. His fur was a rusty-gray color, but mostly red on the backs of the ears and face with a white chin. He had been following his nose through the storm hoping to find the fresh carcass, which he knew was just down stream a ways. However, he realized now that he had been spotted. The intruder turned and dashed upstream heading for the woods. He cursed his bad luck, knowing full well that wolves don't like coyotes.

Unlike the adult wolves, the pups saw the coyote as a playmate. So they ran after coyote to see if he wanted to join in on their fun. Alphie was the first to catch up with the coyote. He tackled the small animal rolling him in the snow several times. By the time the coyote had gotten to his feet, he was surrounded by the wolf pups who were play bowing and barking. The coyote was terrified. Yarrow jumped on the back of the frightened coyote the way she would when playing with her brothers or sister. Coyote freaked! He jumped aside, hunched his body into a half standing curl, lowered his head, bared his teeth, and snarled his angry fear. All five pups leapt back out of reach.

Lupine barked, "Well, that isn't very nice. We're just trying to be friendly."

Coyote did not speak wolf, so her words were lost on him. He backed away from this fearsome pack and scrambled uphill into the woods. The pups did not follow.

Basalt said, "He seemed a little jumpy to me. Maybe he was just having a bad day."

"Maybe," said Alphie, "but this is your lucky day because you're it!" Alphie bumped Basalt into a snowdrift and then ran across the meadow with all the pups behind him. Snow swirled around them like a million moths fluttering toward a distant light. When Alphie reached Cache Creek, which flows into the Lamar River, he turned east and followed the creek upstream. None of the pups thought of the fact that they were in a snowstorm moving further away from their family. By the time they caught up with Alphie, all had forgotten the game of tag. They were leaping over logs of snow and running circles around snow-covered rocks. They sniffed at elk scat under the snow and scent marked here and there to let other animals know that this was part of their territory.

Along an open stretch of the creek, the snowdrifts on the banks had been worn smooth as river rock by the wind. An ice shelf extended over part of the moving water. The ice was free of snow, thin as glass, and so clear that bubbles could be seen rushing below in the fast current. The edge of the blade of ice was jagged and laced with fine designs created by sun, water, and cold, a few of nature's tools. The voice of the creek was a crystal chime.

Alphie listened to the delicate sounds. He was startled when a little gray bird popped up from the fast current, climbed onto the ice, and, while standing in place, did a little dance bobbing up and down staying focused on the lead gray water. The dipper, known to some as a water ouzel, dove back into the freezing water, reappeared with an insect in its beak, and repeated its little dance. Alphie did his own play bow dance. This little bird fascinated Alphie, but the others had already moved on. He followed.

Further upstream, Lupine was the first to stop on the bank of the creek overlooking a pool from which clouds of odorous steam rose into the snowy air. The others joined her. Beyond the fog on the far side of the pool they could see a large bowl-shaped cut in the bank where more stinkwater flowed into the creek. The steam rose; the snow fell. A sputtering gurgle could be heard, which sounded like the very earth itself was growling.

"Where are we?" asked Lupine.

Alphie said, "The bad air coming from under the water is poisonous if you breathe too much of it. Grandfather told me that sometimes cold air traps the warm air, and that bad air can kill any animal unlucky enough to be around to breathe it. He said that our ancestors told a story about a sow grizzly and her three cubs coming in here and all of them died. And then some other bears came in to sniff around and they died as well. The stream over there is Wahb Springs, but the ancestors called this place Death Gulch. Grandfather said that there is a similar place west of the mountains where five bison all died from breathing air near the stinkwater. He also said that some wolves believe that the ghosts of the grizzly bears who died here still roam these woods."

Lupine whispered, "I don't want to run into any ghosts."

"Me neither," said Slate who had tucked his tail and flattened his ears, both signs of fear.

"Don't the ghosts of grizzlies hibernate during the winter?" asked Basalt.

Yarrow said, "That's silly. But this place does give me the creeps!"

"We better get out of here," said Alphie. "Follow me."

Alphie shook snow from his back and head and waded through deep powder following the sound of water running in the warm creek. Basalt, Slate, Yarrow, and Lupine followed in single file. They traveled through the white landscape nose to tail so that they would not lose track of one another. The adventuresome group moved up the narrow valley through a small meadow bordered by thick stands of lodgepole pine trees. Alphie halted mid-meadow when he felt the ground shake. Visibility was poor. He could barely see the woods.

Slate barked, "What was that?"

Emerging from the woods was a huge white form with several more right behind the first. The ground trembled as if the very rock beneath the soil was shifting.

Yarrow screamed, "It's the ghosts of the grizzlies!"

The wolf pups scattered in different directions. Snow exploded in front of the approaching white beasts. Their dark eyes were ringed with snow, and their curved horns framed the snowy manes that covered their heads. Heavy hooves pounded the ground as the ghostly figures stampeded toward the wolves. Alphie took cover behind a nearby log. He peered over the top as the menacing phantoms charged through the meadow.

"Hey," Alphie yelled to the others, "they aren't ghosts! They're bison! Come on over here. Everything's okay."

Basalt and Lupine showed up at Alphie's side. The trio began to howl so that the others could locate them. "Ahoohooohoooooo," they called. And soon the answers came from up the hillside. The three pups moved uphill until they found Yarrow and Slate.

"Are you sure those bison weren't ghosts?" Yarrow asked.

Alphie said, "Ghosts don't smell, and I could sure smell those cows."

Yarrow continued, "Well, if they weren't ghosts then maybe they were spooked by the grizzly ghosts that live here!"

Alphie said, "There are no ghosts up here. You know how some of us have imaginary friends? Well, bison have imaginary enemies. That's why they're always so jumpy and mean. Their own imaginations spooked these bison."

"We shouldn't even be up here by ourselves," said Lupine. "Lets go back to the rendezvous. I bet everyone is worried."

Slate said, "I agree with Lupine. We should head back."

Chapter Seven

Alphie looked around. Many of the nearby trees had disappeared in the snow fog. The wind had increased. Snow swirled around them, and the frigid air whipping through the trees moaned like ghosts. Across the stream, South Cache Creek murmured as it joined Cache Creek. The thin light was draining out of the valley. Soon it would be dark.

"It's not a good idea to travel in a storm like this," said Alphie. "We're miles and miles from home. We better bed down for the night. Maybe the storm will be gone by morning."

They all agreed to sleep out the storm. Among the lodgepole pines was an immense Douglas fir tree. The pups huddled together at its base out of the wind. Snow began to cover them. They would depend on their thick winter coats to keep them warm. One of the pups whispered, "I'm hungry." There was no reply.

Carried on the deep voiced wind were the sounds of trees creaking and branches rubbing their boney hands together. Occasionally there was the thunder crack of a standing dead tree snapping in half and falling through the white darkness to the ground.

Late in the night the wild weather calmed itself as the storm moved off to the east leaving behind several feet of snow. Stars gradually appeared as constellations outlining ancestors from ancient wolf tales. The moon, looking like a river worn rock, rose. Far up the valley, a great horned owl calling its mate broke the silence. "Hooo hoo-hoo hooo hooo." Its mate answered.

The first stain of daylight awoke the pups. They climbed out of their snowy beds, stretched, and shook the white powder from their fur.

Basalt said, "I'm hungry."

"Me, too," said Slate.

Alphie said, "Until we get home, we'll have to settle for mice if you can catch them."

"I could eat a mouse the size of a moose!" said Basalt.

Lupine said, "If we find one that big, we could all eat. Let's go."

Yarrow had already begun plowing her way downhill through the deep snow. The others followed in her tracks forming a line of pups that kept leaping up to see beyond the snowdrifts. Impatient with the slow pace, Alphie bounded through the snow to catch Yarrow. She, too, began to run, as did the others, so that the whole group looked like an avalanche rushing down the mountain. The sun rose a little higher, sending sharp shafts of silver light through the overhead branches. To the west, the moon was about to set behind Mirror Plateau right at the head of Opal Creek. It appeared like a pale piece of ice floating on blue water.

Steam rose from an open stretch of Cache Creek. It froze on the leafless willow branches enclosing each in its own *sheath* of ice. The bright sun bounced off the icy stems, creating a jeweled path along the creek. All of the pups caught up with Yarrow when she stopped by the stream and turned to them.

"Which way do we go?" she asked. "I can't remember."

Alphie said, "Papa told me that if we ever get lost we should follow our own scent trail home. Grandfather said we could follow water home if we're near it. If we went downstream, follow it back up. If we went upstream, which we did, follow it down." He nodded to the right.

Off they went racing through the cold morning, through the deep snow, through the silver light. Each pup dashed through stands of pine, leapt over sage bushes covered with white powder, and pushed each other into windswept drifts. They smelled their own faint scent and that of the ghost bison who had stampeded through the storm.

High above the wolves, near the crest of the mountain, was a long cliff above a steep slope. Deep snow hung over the cliff's edge like a white comforter draped over a bed. The wolves, far below, knew something was wrong when they heard a thunder-like boom crashing down the mountainside. All five pups stopped in their tracks and looked up just in time to see the heavy snow break loose from the cliff. It fell onto the steep slope where more snow began to move down the mountain. The weight and speed of the snow caused trees to snap, each one a rifle shot from the *chaos* of the river of snow. Tree trunks and boulders rolled in the avalanche as it cleared a swath down the mountainside.

Alphie cried out, “Run for it!”

The others could not hear him and stared without moving at the white force rushing toward them. Alphie bumped each one with his chest to get them moving.

“Go! Go! Go!” he shouted. And they went. The five pups ran as they never had before, a blur of wolves moving like the wind through snow. As they sped along the bank of Cache Creek, tons of snow, trees, and boulders crashed onto the valley floor behind them. It shook the earth with a deafening force that would haunt their dreams for weeks to come.

Once they were safe, the pups stopped. Yarrow said, “Oh my, that was close! What’s the mountain so angry about?”

“He’s not angry,” said Alphie. “He’s just shaking snow off his back the way we do.”

Basalt, who was still trying to catch his breath, said, “I’m still hungry.”

“Me, too,” said Slate.

“You two are always hungry,” said Lupine. “Let’s go home. We can eat there.”

Chapter Eight

The pups moved on through woods and fields with Alphie in the lead and Basalt last in line. The others halted when Basalt stopped at the edge of a meadow. He stood intently looking into deep snow. He turned his head as if to listen to the ground in front of him. His ears twitched right and left. Then Basalt rocked back on his hind legs and sprang into the air cutting a perfect arc before landing face first in the deep snow. Only his hind legs and tail were visible. When he emerged from the snow, his teeth were clamped on a fat mouse. He threw the ill-fated mouse in the air and jumped to catch it. He could see Slate approaching so he gave the mouse a few quick bites and swallowed him whole. Slate licked Basalt's muzzle the way he would an adult, hoping that Basalt would cough up the prize. No luck. Slate stared at the snow, cocked his head, and did a dive, which also produced a mouse. He ate it quickly as the others gathered around. For several minutes they all were listening and diving into the snow. Lupine was the only other one to have success. They began to lose interest and, one by one, continued on their way.

The sound of water rushing over stones and murmuring under ice accompanied the pups as they plowed through chest deep, sugary snow. Near Death Gulch, Slate ran ahead of the others. Once out of sight, he hid behind a snowy bush and waited. When the others approached, Yarrow was in the lead. Slate growled like a grizzly bear when she passed the bush. Yarrow yelped, jumped in the air, and rolled over in the snow.

Yarrow snapped at Slate, "That wasn't nice! You nearly scared me to death!"

Slate could not answer because he was laughing so hard. He tried to speak, but just howled harder with laughter. Lupine, Basalt, and Alphie were smiling. They all tackled Slate and began chasing one another in great circles from the creek to the woods. Alphie tripped Basalt. Basalt bumped Yarrow into a drift. She, in turn, pinned her sister against a tall sage bush, causing its burden of snow to fall on top of both wolves.

All five wolves were romping, rolling, barking, and squealing their delight when suddenly from a small ravine, a cow elk jumped up from its bed and bounded down the valley. The startled pups ran in the opposite direction at first, but, then, seeing it was not a grizzly ghost, they chased after the elk.

The elk was running with its head held high as if to say to the pups, 'I'm too healthy for you to catch!' But then she tripped and slid down a slope skidding over snow covered sage bushes. She struggled for a moment before getting back on her feet.

The wolves were getting closer. The cow dashed away from them by *stotting*, which is a kind of hopping that also tells the wolves that she is too healthy for them to take. After a few minutes she changed her *gait* to a prance, racing rapidly to where Cache Creek flowed into the Lamar River. She plunged into a deep pool where ice had not formed. The water was chest high on her. The cow elk turned to face the wolves. Her breath blew out in great puffs of steam. Steam rose from the water, which was warmer than the air. The bright sun turned the water silver, as it curled around the dark coat of the wet elk.

Alphie was the first to reach the bank of the river. He snarled at the elk, but did not go in the water. The hunting lessons from Midnight and others came back to Alphie. He remembered that water is dangerous for wolves. Elk know that wolves are at a great disadvantage in water. This survival technique has saved many elk. Basalt, Lupine, and Slate arrived at the water's edge and bedded, each panting from the chase. Basalt bit at the snow pebbles that had formed on the fur between his toes.

Yarrow was the last to arrive at the river. She, however, did not stop at the edge of the water. She dove full speed into the pool, her splash washing over the elk's head. The surprised elk rose up on her hind legs and came down with her hooves landing on Yarrow. The wolf pup went under, but bobbed up immediately, gasping for air. In an instant Alphie was at her side. He got between the elk and his sister and gently pushed her toward the shore. Both wolves shook water from their fur creating rainbows in the bright sun.

Alphie scolded Yarrow. "Why did you do that? We don't go into water after elk! It's too dangerous!"

"Sorry, Alphie," whimpered Yarrow who was shivering. "I must have missed that lesson. I'll be more careful next time. She really thumped me."

"Are you okay?" Alphie asked.

"Yes. I think so," she said. "I don't think I read that elk very well."

Slate said, "None of us did. She's too strong for us, but, hey, we're still learning."

The elk continued wading back and forth in the deep pool and showed her anger with a sharp trumpet blast causing the pups to flinch.

Lupine said, "The trick for us is to survive each lesson. Isn't that right, Alphie?"

"Right," he said. "But it isn't going to be easy."

The pups began rubbing against each other and wagging their tails and jawing, an affectionate way to hold a neck or shoulder in a tender bite. Basalt liked to give little love nibbles. The pups did a lot of play bowing with chins on the ground and rumps in the air. Then the pups turned away from each other and howled long and deep, a very comforting song for a group of wolf pups out on their own in the wilds of Yellowstone. "Ahoohooohoooooo!" they called. The last thing the pups expected was for their howls to be answered.

Chapter Nine

The pups looked at each other.

"Did you hear that?" Lupine asked.

The others nodded and continued listening. Howls, softer than a whisper, came to them from way up on Mount Norris. "Ahooohooohooooooo," called the distant voices. The howling wolves could not be seen.

"It must be Mother and Papa out looking for us," said Slate. The foggy breath that held his sentence hung in the icy air.

Alphie thought for a moment and then said, "Something doesn't sound right. Why would they sing a 'we are here' howl? If they are looking for us, it should be a 'where are you?' howl."

Yarrow said, "Did you hear that? There's another howl coming from way downstream. Who could that be?"

"The family is just spread out looking for us," Lupine said. "Let's go!" She dashed up the slope away from the river.

Alphie cried out, "No, wait!" But the others had already scampered up after Lupine. The snowy trail she was on zig-zagged up the steep mountainside. Alphie ran after them. He passed Slate who had stopped to sniff the trail of a pine marten. Further on, Alphie pushed Basalt off the trail into deeper snow where he collided with Yarrow, sending her sprawling into another drift. Finally, Alphie reached Lupine. He tackled his sister so that she rolled over on her back. He stood over her and snarled.

"All right already!" she said. "You win!"

The others gathered around Alphie and Lupine, but Alphie remained standing over his sister. The black fur along his neck was up, showing that he was upset. His yellow eyes held the gaze of each of his brothers and sisters.

Alphie said quietly, "We can't rush up the mountain like this. What if those wolves aren't family? Grandfather told me to always use caution when approaching other wolves. We have to make sure they are our pack before we get too close. This isn't play; this is the real thing. We can continue, but you must stay behind me until we're sure that Mother and Papa are up there."

Alphie let Lupine stand up. She shook snow from her coat and said, "You're right, Alphie. I just got excited. I've never been away from home overnight before, and I didn't think."

"I know," said Alphie. "Please follow me."

Once again the pups heard howling from way down the Lamar River. They all turned and looked in that direction. Slate was about to say that the voice sounded like their brother Obsidian, when louder howls poured down on them from above.

In her excitement, Lupine started to howl. Alphie quickly placed a dark paw over her muzzle, something Grandfather had done to him on several occasions. "Shhhhh," he whispered. "Let's see who's up there before we let them know we're here."

Alphie continued up the steep path with the others close behind. The trail went left, then right, and then left again. They passed through a stand of aspen trees that were leafless but thick with new growth. Above the aspen, there were only a few lodgepole pines scattered across the broad, white slope. There was nowhere to hide, no place to take cover. The pups continued beyond the seven thousand foot mark above sea level.

At eight thousand feet Alphie stopped and sniffed a trail that crossed the one they were on. The snow had been plowed and trampled by many animals. The smell of bison was strong, as was the odor of wolves. The wolf smell was unfamiliar to Alphie. He sniffed at a few spots of blood on the trail.

A dark golden eagle cruised by overhead, sliding along an invisible path to the top of the mountain. Several ravens followed the same path. A magpie, with a magnificent tail, flew in the opposite direction with a small string of meat in its beak. He landed far below in a cottonwood tree, where he cached the meat for later use. Way uphill from the pups, a bald eagle kept watch from his *solitary* perch on the limb of a dead tree.

None of these details escaped the notice of Alphie or his brothers and sisters. They knew from numerous lessons that this bird activity meant a carcass was near. The wolves on Mount Norris had made a kill. The pups sniffed the ground and the air. The scent of a fresh kill was faint, but enough to stir their hunger pangs. Slate, Lupine, Yarrow, and Basalt were about to break into a run when Alphie halted them.

“These wolves don’t smell right or sound right,” Alphie said. “We must be careful. If he were with us, that is what Grandfather would say. Hunger bites at me, too, so we’ll take a closer look.”

Alphie led the troop further up the mountain. Above nine thousand feet, they could see a thin forest draped over the bald top of the mountain like a scarf. The smell of bison and wolf were strong. They moved cautiously north toward the great cliff that faced Druid Peak across the valley. Soda Butte Creek flowed silently below.

The snow near the top was windswept and, except for some drifts, not as deep as it was at lower elevations. The large paws of the pups enabled them to move easily over the landscape. The young wolves were side by side when they came to the top of a high knoll. In a low spot below them was the very scene that Alphie had dreaded.

Chapter Ten

Above the bison carcass was a whirlwind of wings flapping around and around. A dozen ravens and as many magpies were on the carcass pecking and pulling at morsels of meat. The golden eagle was perched on one of the horns of the fallen beast. Dozens more birds hopped and squawked around the winter meal, arguing over scraps.

Normally this would have been a welcome sight for hungry pups, however, just beyond the carcass lay three wolves. All had swollen bellies from having eaten so much bison. The two grays were asleep. A large, black wolf was bedded a little closer to the carcass with its head up, facing away from the pups. He seemed busy watching a pair of rust colored coyotes slinking through the woods, in hopes of sharing in the feast.

Basalt whispered, "Hey, Alphie, it looks like the bison's imaginary enemies were real. Those wolves must have spooked the ghost bison that ran past us last night."

"These wolves are not from our pack," Yarrow said. "Who are they?"

Alphie studied the wolves carefully. The black wolf seemed to be one he had seen before. Even the odor of the black now seemed familiar to him. Then he remembered the very scary day on the Mirror Plateau, when he and Grandfather ran into these wolves.

Alphie whispered, "Pelicans. They're from the Pelican Pack. That's Big Black and his buddies. When I was lost last summer, Grandfather was taking me to Opal Creek to find you guys. That's when we ran into these three. They would have killed Grandfather if Mother and Papa hadn't shown up with the rest of the family. These are very dangerous wolves who are even more dangerous now that they have a carcass to defend. We have to get out of here now!"

"I think it's too late," Yarrow said. "Big Black's picked up our scent. He's getting up."

Big Black got to his feet and turned in a circle as he sniffed the air. He was a huge wolf made even bigger by the twenty pounds of bison he had just eaten. He looked up the hill directly at the five pups. Alphie could see blood on his jaws.

Alphie turned away and bounded down the hill with the others close behind. Even though the pups were adult size wolves now, they had no adult experience to help them deal with intruder wolves. Lupine lost her footing and tumbled head over paws before sliding on her belly down a steep snow covered ravine. Alphie nudged her to her feet. They ran on toward the river, toward the Lamar Valley, toward home.

Looking back, Alphie saw Big Black appear at the top of the knoll. His sidekicks were with him when he charged down the hill after the pups. Alphie called out to the others as they ran. "If they get close, we'll have to stand and fight. If that happens, we must stick together. Grandfather said to always take on the leader in a battle." Alphie leaped over a snow covered bush and continued, "Let's cross the river over there!"

Snow dust rose up behind the fleeing pups. Higher on the mountain, snow flew out in all directions as the Pelican Pack trio pounded through deep drifts in pursuit of the pups. The bald eagle perched on the dead tree could see that the distance between Big Black and the pups was diminishing, getting smaller. It appeared as though the dark wolf would overtake the pups before they reached the river. A pair of excited ravens landed in the eagle's tree to watch the unfolding drama.

Alphie already understood that they would not make the river crossing without a fight. He looked way downstream in hopes of seeing Mother, Papa, and Grandfather coming to the rescue. The vast white landscape was empty.

Ahead was a high ridge covered with new growth, short lodgepole pines that had grown up after fire had swept the ridge years earlier. At the top of the ridge Alphie, his brothers, and sisters stopped. He and the others turned to face Big Black and the two grays. The Pelicans were still a hundred yards away running as fast as they could with full bellies.

Alphie howled. The other pups howled, too. "Ahooohooohooooo!" they warned the attackers. The howling surprised the grays who stopped momentarily allowing Big Black to lead the charge on his own.

Alphie spoke rapidly to the others, "Remember, we stick together! We all go after Big Black! It's our only chance!"

The grays continued the chase, but they were way behind Big Black who was just starting up the ridge. The dark fur along his neck was up. He was snarling with teeth bared, and his eyes were like yellow flames.

Alphie plunged down the ridge straight at Big Black. The sudden attack caught the large wolf off guard. He reared up on his hind legs to do a bark-howl, but Alphie was already on him. Alphie bit down on Big Black's shoulder and knocked him over onto his back. Simultaneously, the other pups swarmed over Big Black biting him on the hip, the tail, and one of his hind feet. Big Black tried to get up but was overwhelmed by the pups. He snapped left and right trying to tear at them. The eagle and ravens could hear snarls, growls, and squeals as the wolf pile slid down the side of the ridge.

Big Black gave out a loud yelp when one of the pups bit him on the rump. He managed to leap to his feet and jump clear of the pups. His tail was tucked when he ran past the two grays who skidded to a halt in front of the line of angry pups.

Alphie leaned forward and said, "Boo!"

The two grays bumped into each other as they whirled around and bolted up the hill after Big Black, who was still running as fast as he could.

The five pups howled after the fleeing wolves. It was a victory howl! They began running in circles and play bowing to one another. They climbed on each other forming another wolf pile, alive with wiggling, wagging, and whining. Black fur, white fur, gray, and rust rolled against each other separated here and there by a paw, a thick tail, a pair of ears.

The wild play came to a halt when they heard clear howling from the west. Alphie recognized Grandfather's voice, as well as the worried howls of Mother and Papa. The pups answered the family's call. Together they charged along the river bank through deep snow, crossing their white world, a parade of pups led by Alphie who couldn't wait to tell Grandfather about the Pelican Pack as well as the string of other stories that were part of their winter adventure.

Part 4
Spring

Alphie, the yearling wolf

DRUIDS WATCHING THE DOOMED ELK BULL
LAMAR Canyon.
Fox
Jan 17 '08
DRUIDS HAVE RUN THIS bull elk in + out of Soda Butte Crk all morning
Red fox on the move.
480

Chapter One

Druid Peak stood as a sentinel, rising a few thousand feet above Lamar Valley. Its basalt cliffs were high, gray rock etched with late May snow. Above, the peak was framed by deep blue sky, while below, across its lap, an apron of forest hid a jumble of ancient boulders that during some distant quake had tumbled from the mountain top, gathering there like the remains of a fallen castle. Back then, on that prehistoric day, the startling thunder created by that avalanche filled the valley for a brief moment, as if it were a boiling lake of terrible sound. Now, the large boulders were lichen-covered with lodgepole pines growing from cracks in the rock. Some tree roots snaked over the rock in search of soil. While the cliffs above were drenched in the gold light of the sun rising over Mount Norris across the valley, the rocks below wore a softer light, filtered by the forest canopy. Where boulder leaned against boulder, caves formed. Some were shallow shelters, others deep enough for a wolf's den.

As it happened, there were two active dens in and near the rocks. Just downslope from the labyrinth of fallen rocks, a den had been dug under an old Douglas Fir. Roots, like a tangle of snakes, held the walls and ceiling in place. Four feet into the long, dark chamber, Pearlyeverlasting lay curled up with her three pups. She was almost as white a wolf as her flower namesake. Having just nursed, her pups, a gray and two blacks, stretched and mewed softly in their sleep. At age two, Pearly, as Alphie liked to call her, had dispersed from her Lamar

Valley Pack, and returned home alone when she was ready to have her pups. This was not an uncommon story among dispersing females in Yellowstone National Park. If the territory required to begin a new pack was limited, wolves like Pearly headed for home. Her family not only welcomed her back, the pack adopted her pups as if they were their own.

Among the boulders above Pearly's den, Alphie, the black wolf with the crescent moon on his chest, was lying down with his head erect and attentive. Half asleep next to him was Grandfather. As a yearling, Alphie was now as big as his grandfather. They were both near the entrance to the second den, belonging to Mother Wolf. Grandfather lifted his silver head when he heard Alphie whine.

"What is it, Alphie?" he asked.

"Mother won't let me near the den," Alphie said. "Every time I get close to see the puppies, she growls and snaps at me."

Grandfather said, "She's just trying to protect those babies. She did the same for you when you were just a pup, as my mother did for me. Maybe if you brought her more food or found something the young ones could play with, she might be more tolerant."

"I just want to see them," Alphie said. "Why doesn't she bring them out of the den? Let them play a little?"

"She'll do that soon. They're getting big by now. With all five of them in there with Mother, it must be getting a little crowded," Grandfather said.

Alphie's ears stiffened. Sharp, high-pitched barks came from the dark rock cave where Mother Wolf groomed her pups. In the dim light, the four grays and the black climbed over each other and mother attempting to play in the tight quarters. As some yelps and squeals were heard, Alphie jumped up and cautiously crossed the flat ground in front of the cave entrance. He looked left and right of the entrance at several sleeping adults. They did not stir. When Alphie poked his head into the den, he was greeted with a low growl. He backed away. Then he did a jump left and a jump right and a play bow in front of the cave. The cave was silent.

Almost as if he had just remembered something, Alphie whirled around and dashed down the hillside. He leapt over low rocks and blowdowns, fallen trees pushed over by fists of wind. Where the sloped earth was exposed to the sun, bushes were budding and the green stalks of flowers were pushing upward. Alphie left large tracks in the thawed earth. He also left tracks in ravines where the snow remained, granular and deep, shaded there from the warmth of the sun. Alphie's breath was visible in the cold morning air.

Not far from where the forest thinned to a few scattered pines, low in the valley near a long dead fir tree above an eyebrow of rock, Alphie found the old elk carcass. Most of the meat had been consumed by his pack weeks ago. Also, the many scavengers who depend on the wolf had visited the kill: eagles, ravens, magpies, coyotes, and foxes to name a few. Alphie tugged at the scattered remains as the bull looked on with empty eyes. Shredded elk hide and tufts of fur clung to rocks and bushes. Much of the fur had been eaten because it wraps itself around bone shards to ease those slivers through the wolf's intestines. Deep inside the rib cage of the carcass, Alphie found one last treasure, a rag of meat still attached to the spine. He chewed it loose, and, holding it draped in his jaws, he trotted uphill toward the den site.

Alphie passed through a stand of lodgepole pines. Wild onion stalks had sprouted in the soft earth and perfumed the air. There were cut poles, twenty feet in length, leaning against larger, living trees. Many poles sagged with age. Grandfather had explained that human beings had used those poles to make their mountain shaped lodges. Each year when they left, they took their hides with them, but not the poles. "For more generations than our ancestors can remember," Grandfather had said, "the Crow beings have not returned. The same is true with many things in the forest. Animals disappear; whole packs go missing. Many things are temporary, even you and me." The young wolf recalled Grandfather's words as he trotted further up Druid Peak.

Alphie was ascending the final steep slope below Pearly's den when he heard the howl. It was not an alarm call or the calling together of the family. It was a howl of mourning, a howl to accompany a wolf's spirit when it leaves the pack. "Grandfather," Alphie whispered to himself.

He dashed past Pearly's den with the slab of meat flapping in his jaws. There, in front of Mother Wolf's den, the whole pack was gathered. Father Wolf was still howling. Alphie's brothers and sisters had returned from a hunt and were sitting still and silent. All the pack was there including Grandfather. Grandfather signaled to Alphie to come sit by him. Alphie did so.

Pearly's puppies were out of the den and had joined Mother Wolf's puppies. All eight were playing in front of the den opening, five grays and three blacks. Their small faces looked startled as they ran in circles, jumped each other, and chewed on an elk antler that Papa Wolf had dragged home. One of Mother Wolf's pups, a large black with huge feet, approached Alphie and stole the slab of meat from his jaws. All the other pups jumped the black one and began a tug of war. With all the play, Alphie could not see why Papa Wolf mourned so.

"Grandfather," he started to say.

Grandfather leaned close to Alphie and said, “Shhhhh. Look there.” He nodded toward the cave entrance.

Mother Wolf was lying down with her front paws extended. Between them was another pup. It was a tiny gray, half the size of the others. It struggled to stand, but fell, quivering, onto its side. Mother Wolf tried to help it by nudging the little wolf with her nose, but it just slid in the dust. Alphie could see its small chest rising and falling rapidly. Another pup ran toward the helpless one, but Mother Wolf snarled. The pup retreated.

Within a few minutes the chest of the frail pup stopped moving. Mother Wolf nudged it a few more times. When she got no response, she stood and quietly picked up the dead pup in her jaws. The others watched as she carried the limp body above the boulder field to an open area of soft dirt. With Papa Wolf's howls filling the forest, she laid the pup near a sage bush and began digging. Dirt sprayed behind her. Papa continued his death song. The others joined in, so that the whole valley was filled with their sorrowful voices. Even the pups became still and tried to sing. Once the hole was deep enough, Mother placed her pup in the ground and covered her over. She joined in the howling.

“What happened?” asked Alphie.

Grandfather said, “We didn't even know that that pup was in the den. She was so small. Some wolves are born with a weak life force, the urge to live that gives them the will to fight for food. Life is hard for all living things, and if you don't come into the world with a strong will, chances are you won't make it. As a pack we can protect pups against things that may try to destroy them: cats, bears, eagles; but if the light within is dim, we have no power to make it brighter. These other pups are strong. They have a good chance of survival, if they don't get killed by predators or get lost.”

Alphie looked directly at Grandfather. He knew that Grandfather was referring to the time when Alphie had been separated from the pack when he was just a pup. Once again Alphie learned how uncertain life could be.

Mother Wolf returned to her family. She lay on her side in front of the den and allowed the eight pups to leap on her, tug on her tail, pull on her ears, and cover her with their wriggling life. She groomed one pup by licking it all over while it squirmed to get free of the paw that pinned it. Several pups began to nurse. And before long, they were all fighting for food.

Chapter Two

As the sun rose and set, rose and set, and days passed, wolves left the den area in pairs or alone to scour the countryside for prey. Even though the pups were still nursing, they had started to eat some regurgitated food. When a pack member returned with a full belly, the pups would mob their older brother or sister, licking them on the lips and face in an attempt to trigger a regurgitation. If successful, the pups would dive into the warm stew, devour it, and lick each other clean. They were always hungry.

On this particular day, Alphie left the den site before daylight. He took the Ledge Trail from which he could see the confluence of Soda Butte Creek and the Lamar River, and much of the valley floor between Mount Norris and Specimen Ridge. He continued west, loping across snow fields and long meadows free of snow. When he headed downslope to the Lamar River, the faintest light was just beginning to stain the sky, causing stars to dim. He had caught a whiff of something, an odor so faint that it was barely detectable. The smell grew stronger as he waded into the fast water of the river. Where the stream bends through the cottonwood trees, its pools are deep. Alphie swam to the far side and emerged onto a stony beach. There he shook, rolling to the left and right, shedding water in a misty spray. Looking on from a cottonwood branch, a bald eagle with a serious face watched the black wolf move through sage and new grass. A red fox moved on quick feet over drift wood logs, hoping to escape the notice of the dark wolf moving toward him. Fortunately, the larger canid was following his nose, not his eyes. Alphie continued west along the tree line. He stopped for several minutes near an *alluvial fan*, a 'v' shaped meadow that cut into the edge of the forest. The odor he was following grew weaker causing him to backtrack. Once he regained the scent, Alphie moved more quickly, trotting past Amethyst Creek where a waterfall gurgled. A raven was flying ahead of Alphie as if he were leading the black wolf to food. Alphie could hear many ravens arguing in a cluster of pines beside a trail that led up the east flank of Jasper Bench.

As Alphie approached the trees, he could see the large, dark bison carcass. The bull was a winter kill meaning that it had not been strong enough to endure the bitterly cold, snowy winter. Now ravens were dancing around the fallen giant, pecking and flapping at each other, their voices creating a *cacophony* of sound. Ravens, Alphie knew, needed wolves to open a carcass so that they could feed. Many of these ravens, he already knew. They had been playmates near the den and the rendezvous when he was a pup, and had been escorts of his on several adventures. A few of the ravens had helped him find food before, a *symbiotic relationship* that worked to the benefit of both raven and wolf.

The bison hide was tough and frozen, but Alphie was able to peel it back enough to feed. The bald eagle had glided in and waited his turn on a branch above the carcass. A magpie perched on one of the bison's horns. A hundred yards uphill from the cluster of trees sat a pair of coyotes, barking at the young wolf. Not only did the coyotes want to feed for themselves, they had hungry pups of their own in a den up on Jasper Bench.

Once Alphie had eaten his fill, he laid on top of the dark mound of the carcass, rolled onto his back, and squirmed from one side to the other. Slowly he slid off the carcass onto his head. Then he pushed sideways back onto the carcass. He was adorning himself with the scent of bison. Squawks and barks accompanied his every move. Finally, Alphie headed home with a full belly and smelling like a bison.

Back at the den Pearly's pups were playing with Mother Wolf's pups. When the pups were hungry, their mothers were not too particular about which pups they nursed. When Alphie arrived, he was overrun by all eight pups. They licked his muzzle, his eyes, his legs, whatever they could reach. They mewed and yipped and jumped against their big, dark brother. The puppies' wide eyes were blue flames. Alphie lowered his head and regurgitated the bison stew. The pups attacked the warm mass of partially digested meat. They stepped in it, fell in it, were pushed face first into the steaming broth. After it was gone they licked each other to get every morsel.

Lupine and Yarrow, Alphie's dark gray sisters, returned to the den with empty bellies. The pups tried to get them to regurgitate, but they had nothing to give. The sisters began sniffing Alphie. Even though they were smaller than Alphie, they could still jump on him and knock him over, which is exactly what they did. They sniffed him everywhere and licked his fur. The bison smell was strong and made their bellies growl. Alphie did not have to say that he had found a carcass; they knew. The odor told the tale.

Alphie untangled himself from their attentions and bolted down slope past Pearly's den. His sisters followed. They raced along the Ledge Trail, the meadow ridge, and the snowy ravines. They descended to the flats and swam across the swift, muddy water of the Lamar River. Snow melt in the mountains made the water deep, fast, and full of *sediment*. They stopped for a moment to watch a cinnamon black bear next to a rotted log. The round bear sniffed the length of the log. He returned to the middle, stood up on his hind legs, and came down hard on the old tree trunk with his front paws. He repeated the action several times, *pulverizing* the soft wood. While the bear lapped up delicious red ants with his long, pink tongue, the three yearling wolves continued on across the open sage flats past Amethyst Creek.

Lupine, Yarrow, and Alphie stopped suddenly. Several dozen bison were lined up nose to tail, single file, in a line that stretched up the hillside. Heads were held low; ropey tails flicked their tassels back and forth shooing flies. The short body hair revealed iron muscles, and the curly, black wool surrounding each massive head was a nest for the dark, stone eyes. One at a time they would step up to the carcass of the old bull, sniff at it, nudge it lightly, or lick it. It was as if each bison were paying its respects to their dead brother. The coyotes had been chased off and were bedded on the bench near Jasper Creek. The ravens were dark silhouettes, complaining among the pine boughs. The eagle had retreated to a dead cottonwood down by the river.

Alphie decided not to be *deterred* by the wall of bison. Lupine and Yarrow felt more *intimidated* and stayed put. When Alphie approached the large bull at the head of the line, the bison's tail went straight up. The young wolf understood the warning. Grandfather had said that the raised tail meant charge or discharge. Discharge meant poop. This bull, however, was angry; he was telling Alphie to back off. Alphie's tucked tail revealed his nervousness. He even flattened his ears a little. But he didn't move back; he moved forward. The big bull snorted and a rippling grumble went along the line of bison like a sound wave. Alphie halted a moment, then stepped up to the carcass.

The bull exploded in a fury, lunging at the black intruder with his head low. This bison had killed wolves before. He knew how to use his horns, knew how to kick, knew how to stomp a nuisance wolf into the ground. Alphie was startled to see the bison move so quickly. He was just barely able to leap to one side. The ravens lifted from their branches, squawking, and then resettled to watch the drama below. The bison snorted and swung its dark head at the wolf. Alphie dashed down the slope. His sisters had already retreated to the river bank. Six more bison joined the bull, running stiff-legged toward Alphie. Alphie had just run a short way before the bison broke off the chase and returned to their place in line.

Alphie walked over to his sisters and bedded between them.

Yarrow said, "Look." She motioned with her head for Alphie to look up at Jasper Bench. Working their way down toward the carcass were the two coyotes Alphie had seen earlier.

"Grandfather should see this," Alphie said.

Lupine said, "He's babysitting the pups this morning. Mother and Pearly are on a hunt with the others."

"This is the first time they have been away from the pups," said Yarrow.

Alphie said, "Still, it's too bad Grandfather will miss all the fun. He likes to watch when coyotes have a bad day."

The three wolves watched as the coyotes approached the line of bison. Bison tails went up as the coyotes crept closer to the carcass. Even though their hunger was stronger than their fear of the bison, the coyotes were still cautious, each muscle ready to snap like a spring if the hairy beasts challenged them.

Alphie and his sisters moved in for a closer view. They bedded just fifty yards away. The coyotes stood still near the carcass as the bison's verbal warnings grew stronger. The pair twitched their rust colored ears and inhaled the tempting odor of the dead animal. The larger of the two coyotes, a thirty-five pound male, stepped forward and bit a flap of loose skin on the belly of the dead bison. Several bison snorted loudly and charged. Both coyotes yelped and practically turned inside out trying to avoid the stomping hooves and gouging horns. The female coyote managed to make a perfect paw print that looked like a fossil in a fresh, greenish-brown bison patty, which was still warm and sticky. The pair ran back along the line of bison. Each bison they passed turned and joined the charge. The air vibrated with the thunder of hooves and angry bellowing. The coyotes doubled their speed as the *disgruntled* herd chased them up the slope.

Alphie said, "This is great! Let's go!"

The wolves moved in on the carcass and fed as rapidly as they could. Before long they could hear the thud of hooves drawing near. Off they went like gusts of wind across the flats, across the river. On the north side of the river the sun made rainbows in the spray of water created when all three wolves shook from side to side. They looked back and saw that the bison had turned back to continue the tribute to their fallen brother. The coyotes were high on Jasper Bench barking at a safe distance from the bison. Alphie, Lupine, and Yarrow turned north and trotted toward the distant Den Forest.

Chapter Three

Many days later after the bison carcass was gone, the pack once more roamed the valley in search of food for the hungry pups. Very early one morning as night was ending, the moon, a brilliant white plate, was setting to the west of Lamar Valley. To the east the cold fire of the sun began flooding the valley. Between the sun and the moon were the wolves, moving out of the Den Forest toward the confluence of the Lamar River and Soda Butte Creek.

During the night, most of the adults in the pack had returned to the den with empty stomachs. As much as the puppies licked the muzzles of those hunters, their begging for food was in *vain*; the adults had nothing to give. Now it was Alphie's turn to lead his sisters and brothers on a hunt. The line of wolves that moved toward the valley was led by Alphie with Basalt and Slate, the grays, close behind. They were followed by Yarrow, Obsidian, and Lupine, all of which were beginning to lose their winter coats. They looked as if they had been in a fight or had fallen in a creek and slept with wet fur. Never-the-less, they trotted proudly into the valley. Trailing way behind was Grandfather. The hunt had been his idea. He saw how worn down the other adults were and how hungry the pups were, so he told the yearlings that it was up to them to hunt.

These hunters had a few problems. Often Alphie had to stop and wait for Grandfather to catch up. Just recently the old wolf seemed to get much older and slower. It was difficult for him to keep up the pace of the yearlings. Alphie had noticed that rather than going on hunts, Grandfather seemed content to hang around the den with the new puppies.

A second problem was that even though Alphie and his siblings were now yearlings, they still had a lot of puppy in them. When they stopped to wait for Grandfather, chaos broke out. During one of their early stops, Yarrow and Lupine jumped on Slate, Basalt picked a fight with a stick, and Obsidian chased a Uinta ground squirrel. Alphie tried to keep everyone focused on the task at hand, but he, too, joined the play. He pounced on the squirrel that Obsidian was chasing and tossed the terrified thing in the air like a toy. Obsidian tried to catch it on the fly, but the fortunate squirrel landed near a hole and managed to scramble into a tunnel. Obsidian began digging feverishly spraying dirt onto Yarrow, Lupine, and Slate. The three dashed out of range and tackled Alphie who had just pushed Basalt onto his back. The yearlings squealed and growled in their rough play, while Obsidian, having abandoned the squirrel, danced around the tangled wolves play bowing. With front legs forward, head down, rump up, he hopped back and forth.

Grandfather appeared. In the bright sunlight his fur seemed almost white. He said, "Are you youngsters ready to continue, or do I have to keep waiting for you?" He smiled.

Alphie said, "We were just waiting for you!"

"That's what it looks like," he said. "Don't worry about me. If you find an elk, I'll be there to help you bring it down."

"We weren't worried about you, Grandfather," said Lupine. "We just wanted to do this!" Lupine leapt onto Grandfather knocking him onto his side. The others jumped on the old wolf, as well. They jawed and pawed at Grandfather and each other. There was a lot of licking and tail wagging. Grandfather managed to get a long leg around Alphie's neck and wrestled him to the ground. The friendly family tussle continued for several minutes strengthening their bond to one another. It was that bond that was the foundation of the pack. Out of it grew caring and courage, equal tools for survival.

Finally, Alphie turned toward Soda Butte Creek. The others lined up behind him with Grandfather way in the rear. As they moved, there was still a little shoving within the line, but gradually they settled down and began the hunt in *earnest*. They read the wind for the scent of elk. They listened for the shuffle of hooves or the muffled conversation of the herd. Their eyes were alert to anything that moved.

Lupine spotted dirt flying like a fountain off the trail beyond a sage bush and loped over to sniff around. She barked and jumped to one side when confronted by a badger. Alphie and the others came running. They surrounded the animal, which, at first, flattened itself against the ground. Its gray body was flattened out; its black and white head was erect. His eyes were squinted in anger at this intrusion on its hunt. When Slate stretched out his paw and touched the badger's back, the badger exploded in a furious assault. He was a blur spinning around and around, snarling, hissing, and growling. Its bared teeth clicked as it snapped at each intruder.

The wolves leapt back in surprise at the fury of this angry little creature. The yearling wolves just wanted to play. They danced around the badger delighted with his fiery temper. Alphie and the others barked, did play bows, and made false lunges at the badger. His masked face flashed his displeasure to the right, the left, then right again.

When Grandfather caught up with the yearlings, he said, "I think we better leave this guy alone. He's already having a hard time without us. Look over there." The young wolves attention had been so focused on the badger, that they hadn't noticed the coyote. The badger had been trying to dig up a ground squirrel that had disappeared into its narrow burrow. The squirrel had escaped out another entrance a few dozen feet away where the coyote was waiting. As the wolves looked on, the coyote was prancing away with the limp ground squirrel hanging from its jaws. The back of the coyote's ears were a rusty-red, and his thick tail was out straight and confident. Grandfather continued, "Very tricky coyote. He probably has young to feed back in his den. I'm sure badger has young, too. Why don't we leave him alone and go after a bigger meal."

Alphie gave the badger one last poke just to rile him up. The badger snarled and retreated into the dense sage. Unaware that the squirrel was already gone, he continued to dig. Grandfather trotted off toward the creek. The others followed.

Chapter Four

The hunting party of seven wolves moved along a trail that had been used by bison, elk, antelope, grizzly bears, and other wolves for *millennia*. These Lamar wolves were characters in a play that had been written thousands of years ago, the same *ancestral* drama enacted by the first wolves. The ending was always uncertain. The old stories of the hunt that Grandfather carried with him were the same ones that were beginning to grow in the hearts of the yearlings that trailed behind him. Twice he paused to tell them, first, about a hunt along the cliffs of Mount Norris and, second, about a Lamar River stand-off with a bull elk as told to him by his grandfather. He also stopped for other stories, as well. Some ended in failure or tragedy, while some were successful. The stories taught that many, hunting as one, was the way to success and that every hunt had its risks.

Due to snowmelt in the mountains, the water in Soda Butte Creek was high and fast. The rush of water over rock and the scent of muddy pools swirling with debris triggered in each wolf the memory of their first Crossing as pups. For Alphie and his siblings, it was just short of a year ago when they moved from the den to the rendezvous site. The high water was so terrifying then because they were so small. Alphie remembered that Mother Wolf had carried him across in her jaws. Now he and the others had long legs and were as big as Grandfather. This crossing would be easy. They plunged into the frigid water.

Grandfather shook off on the far side and waited until the others were safely across. Lupine, the smallest of the yearlings, had floated around a bend, but soon came bounding through the low grass where the others waited on a high knoll. They had a group rally rubbing against each other, licking faces, and whining their joy, which led to a family howl that put the whole valley on notice that they were there. South of them on the grassy flats, bordered to the west by the Lamar River, elk lifted their heads. A dozen bulls began to move up the slope of Mount Norris, their giant antlers still in velvet. The fur of their massive bodies was the color of dried grass, their rumps an off white, and the rough mane along their necks, dark as wet pine bark. The long face of each elk was serious and attentive. Just above a thick grove of young pines, the elk huddled close together, looking in all directions. They had not seen the wolves yet, but they had heard them and smelled them.

Alphie led his brothers and sisters off the knoll and across the flats. Grandfather stayed put while the others spread out. The plan was to charge the elk. Once they were on the run, the wolves would be able to see if any of the bulls had a weakness. They were looking for an old bull or one that was malnourished after the long winter or one that had a bad leg that would slow him down. Grandfather's plan was to remain bedded and watch the hunt. If one of the elk happened to run his way, he would do his best to bring it down or turn it back toward the younger wolves.

Yarrow and Lupine tried to stay close to Alphie as he climbed Mount Norris to get above the elk. Basalt, Obsidian, and Slate took a more direct route. The three brothers bedded a hundred yards downslope from the nervous elk, each of which could now clearly see the wolves. Alphie and his sisters bedded above the herd and began to howl. "Ahooohooooh ooooo," they sang. Like a flock of birds all turning simultaneously in the sky, the elk turned uphill to face the bedded trio.

The three brothers below answered the howl with howls of their own. "Ahooohooooh ooooo," they replied. The elk shuffled their hooves and faced downhill. They began to push closer together. A few stomped their front feet. There was some grumbling among the elk, some snorting and huffing. Alphie knew that the elk were wound tight and ready to bolt away from their *predicament*. As if a silent signal had been sent among the wolves, they all attacked at the same time. The yearlings snarled and bared their teeth as they charged. Alphie held his tail high, like an alpha wolf, as he attacked. His confidence passed through the elk herd like a shock wave.

Confusion and panic broke out in the herd. The elk whirled in circles, banging into one another in their attempt to escape the wolf assault. One large bull charged the three brothers, causing them to hesitate long enough for the herd to bolt south across the open fields toward Cache Creek. All of the elk stampeded in that direction, their hooves thudding on the ground like muffled drums. They were faster than the wolves and were pulling away from their pursuers when they ran into Yarrow. She had anticipated their escape route and had gotten out in front of them. She ran full speed at the lead bull. When he turned west toward the Lamar River, the others followed.

As the elk ran across the landscape, the wolves watched the gait of each one, listened to their labored breathing, and sniffed the air for the odor that signals a sick animal. Alphie chose a bull that moved a little slower than the others. He snapped at its hind legs in an attempt to cut it from the herd. The bull broke from the herd and turned toward the knoll, a thousand yards away, where Grandfather was bedded.

While Lupine and Yarrow kept after the herd, Alphie and his brothers tested the single bull. As the wolves raced across the flats, they read the elk to determine if he was weak enough to take down. They knew that this was the situation described by Grandfather, where the risk was life or death. They knew that wolves before them had been killed during a hunt, impaled by antlers or kicked by hooves.

Slate was the first to make contact. He bit the elk on the left hind leg. The bull kicked Slate, gave him a glancing blow with both hooves which sent the young wolf rolling over in the grass. Slate had yelped on impact, but now scrambled to his feet and rejoined the chase. The elk had already run half the distance to Grandfather. The bull pranced with his head held high in an attempt to convince the wolves that he was too healthy for them to take. The old wolf stood up and stretched. He watched as Alphie made contact with the bull. Alphie snapped at the right side of the elk, coming away with a mouthful of fur. The elk kicked at air, bucked, and sped up as it approached the knoll.

Grandfather gave out a primitive growl as he charged the bull. The bull lowered his head and charged Grandfather. Even though the velvet covered antlers posed little threat, the old wolf broke to the right keeping the bulls attention until Alphie and his brothers arrived. As is true with many predators, it is the running of prey that triggers the chase in them. When the elk stopped, the wolves stopped. Obsidian and Slate even bedded. All were breathing hard. Three bison and an antelope near the creek were watching the drama, as were dark hungry-eyed ravens that gathered in nearby cottonwood trees.

Grandfather said to Alphie, "Did you have to pick such a big one? He looks strong to me."

"He was a lot slower than the others," Alphie said. "Also, he's got that bad smell about him. Do you smell it?"

"Yes, you're right," Grandfather said sniffing the air.

Alphie said, "I think this one has troubles."

Alphie lunged at the bull to get him to run again. The elk held his ground and lowered his head. Alphie backed away. Basalt attacked from the rear, but had to dance to the side when the bull kicked at him. Grandfather wandered closer to the elk being careful not to make eye contact. He was actually looking away from the huge animal, when, without warning, Grandfather turned and leapt for the long neck of the elk. The bull was so startled that he raised up and almost stomped Grandfather who had jumped to one side. When the elk's hooves hit the ground, he broke into a run heading for the Lamar River.

The four young wolves charged after the elk. Grandfather did as well, but he took his time. He did call after the yearlings, "Don't let him get in the river!" However, the call came too late. The bull plunged into the icy stream; water exploded in a tremendous spray ahead of him. Lupine and Yarrow had finally joined the chase, but they halted on the river bank with their brothers. Yarrow remembered her icy plunge into the waters of Cache Creek in the dead of winter, when she was chasing a cow elk that had taken refuge there. The near death experience was still fresh in her mind. Best not to make the same mistake twice.

Yarrow did pace up and down the bank with her sister. Alphie and Slate bedded close to the water. Basalt and Obsidian went upstream to the rapids and crossed the Lamar. When the pair bedded across the stream from Alphie and the others, the bull moved away from the shore into belly-deep water. The brown water swirled around the animal sucking at its body heat, at its strength.

Grandfather arrived. He had seen standoffs like this many times. It could last for hours or days. As long as the old bull stayed in the water, he had the advantage. He knew it; the wolves knew it. But the yearlings were restless. Even though Grandfather bedded, all of the others were now up and pacing. Lupine had crossed upstream and joined her brothers on the other side. She waded a little way into the stream. The bull charged her, kicking forward with his deadly hooves. She dashed up on shore, as if she were attempting to lure him out. The bull moved back into deep water and continued holding his head high. Facing upstream, the elk was vigilant, looking left and right to keep track of all the wolves.

Grandfather said, "You all should relax. Get some rest. This will take time and patience. Take turns giving him grief. That way we will be fresh when he makes a run for it."

The yearlings tried to settle down. However, soon they were rolling on their backs, then poking each other with their paws, then finding sticks to chew, then stealing each others' sticks, then chasing each other in circles, then tackling one another. The elk misunderstood the play and thought the wolves were getting ready to charge. He moved to shallow water, stomped his feet, and blew air out of his nose in a threatening wheeze. All of the wolves went on alert, even Grandfather. Lupine was already in the water when Grandfather plunged into the deep pool and swam directly toward the bull. Alphie and Slate were right behind him. They hoped to intimidate the elk, forcing him out of the river. To the elk, Lupine, Obsidian, and Basalt posed a greater threat. He moved back to deeper water where he faced Grandfather. Grandfather could not get good footing in the deep water, but attempted anyway to go in for the kill. The panicked elk rose up on its hind legs, and, in a flash, stomped Grandfather so hard that he disappeared under the water.

Alphie cried out, "Grandfather!"

The old wolf surfaced and swam weakly back toward shore. Alphie got downstream of Grandfather. The swift current pushed the old wolf against Alphie who helped him to the rocky shallows. Meanwhile, the bull rushed out of the river and headed west. He climbed a low spot on the old riverbed and disappeared. Alphie's brothers and sisters followed. Grandfather bedded on the grassy bank. He winced at the pain and panted rapidly.

"Will you be okay?" asked Alphie.

"I think something inside may be broken," he whispered. "That bull thumped me good. You know, Alphie, it's a terrible trick of Nature that our minds and hearts don't age like the body does. For a moment there, I thought I was one of you, a young and strong yearling. My heart even told me I was, but it was wrong. Even so, it was a good feeling." The old wolf tried to smile, but shuddered instead. "I'll be fine," he finally said. "You go on with the others. I'll just rest right here for a while. I think you were right about this bull; he did smell bad." Alphie swam the river, shook off, and dashed off to the west to find the others who were still pursuing the bull.

The sun slid all the way to the western end of the valley and was a blaze of red, when Alphie and Yarrow arrived back at the river crossing where they had left Grandfather. Both wolves had traces of blood on their faces and full bellies. The others, likewise in appearance, were strung out behind them in a line all the way to Amethyst Creek. The two yearlings crossed the river. Grandfather was not there.

Back at the den, after Alphie had regurgitated for the excited pups, he asked Mother Wolf, "Have you seen Grandfather?"

"No, Alphie," she said. "I thought he was with you."

Alphie described the battle with the bull elk in the river and described how Grandfather had gotten hurt.

Mother Wolf said, "I'm sure he'll be fine. Grandfather has just gone off to rest somewhere. He'll come home when he's ready. By the way, I'll be going to your kill in the morning with the rest of the pack while you watch the puppies. Pearly will be with me, so you'll have her's, too. It would be best if you don't lose any of them.

Chapter Five

Compared to the short frozen days of winter, these spring days were warm. Yet the nights were cold enough to cover still water with a skin of ice. In the morning before sunup, when light began to fill the sky and the moon had set, Druid Pond, a small piece of water that lay hidden below the Den Forest, was rimmed with ice. Intricate designs of flowers, stalks of grass, and prisms of glass decorated the new ice along the edge of the pond. The ice extended just a few feet from shore, where it gave way to dark water that lay still as a mirror in the windless morning. The reflection of a few bright stars lingered on the surface.

During the night, many animals visited this watering hole. A mountain lion had moved down from the cliffs and crouched by the shore with its tail snaking through the air. Its pink tongue lapped water, some of which dripped from its chin onto the ice. A black bear with two *coy* had sniffed along the shore and then drank, before moving like a trio of shadows into the forest. A bull moose with velvet antlers had stood knee deep in the pond and slurped water. He used his long face to locate green shoots below the surface. When he waded out, the new ice clinked like a row of chimes. He browsed a cluster of budding willows before moving on.

In the hushed silence, foot steps could now be heard. The whisper of moving grass, the snap of a twig, the slip of an uncertain paw announced the approach of wolf pups. There were several narrow chutes of grass that reached into the forest like fingers. Low in one of the chutes was a 'v' tree, one tree, two trunks. The sage rustled near the tree. There was a thin wash of light in the sky. The oval pond was glass. The first to emerge from the thicket of sage was a black pup whose blue eyes were wide and alert. It was the first time he had seen the sky unbroken by trees. This new world beyond the forest was immense and frightening. His small ears searched for sound. A solitary sandhill crane feeding in the grass on the far side of the pond leapt into the air with a screech, its wings flapping wildly. The black pup rushed back to the sage and huddled there with the others. The bird glided across the valley and settled south of Soda Butte Creek.

The pups were whining and pushing closer together. Pearly's pups were there, as well, and added to the number of wagging tails, jawing mouths, paws on faces, and twitching ears. Alphie was bedded next to them. As the babysitter for the day, he was in charge; he was responsible for all the pups. The black yearling was on full alert.

Finally, Alphie stood and moved toward the pond. The puppies unraveled themselves and ran after him. As the pups investigated the ice and water, Alphie sniffed around the perimeter of the pond. He smelled faint cat scent and bear and moose, as well as bison and bird. He was satisfied, though, that the odors were weak, indicating that the threats had departed.

Alphie bedded near the pups and watched them play. One black growled at its reflection on the ice. A gray broke the edge of the ice and fell into the dark, cold water. Alphie jumped to the rescue and pulled the drenched pup onto the shore. He attempted to lick it off, but the pup would not hold still.

Once Alphie bedded again, two pups climbed on him. After a while, they tried to nurse. Alphie smiled and gently pushed them away. "You'll have to wait for Pearly and Mother," he whispered.

The pups explored excitedly along the shore. A mountain bluebird took flight, looking like a piece of sky that has broken loose and drifted like a blue leaf over the sage, where it landed and resumed its soft warbling notes. One of the gray pups attacked a new green shoot of an arrowleaf balsamroot, while a second gray growled at a dark rock sticking above the ice. One of the black pups sat on the edge of the ice and poked at his reflection in the water with his paw.

An alarm call from a black pup that had wandered too far down the shore brought Alphie to his feet. He and the other pups ran to see what the danger might be. The little black jumped from side to side and barked at something in the brush. Alphie saw that it was a bull elk skull suspended between sage bushes by its immense antlers. The skinless skull had empty eye sockets and exposed teeth. All of the pups started to growl and bark. Alphie realized that they thought that it was still alive. He attacked the skull, pushed it to the ground, and shook it viciously. His snarls startled the pups. They scattered in every direction. Within moments, satisfied that Alphie had killed the dead elk, they returned. Each pup imitated Alphie by attacking the skull. While pulling on the tines of the antlers, they managed to roll the skull over on top of themselves. The terrified puppies ran off once again.

The puppy play continued as they began to tackle each other. A black had his sister's leg in his mouth. She gripped a tail in her teeth. A gray was helplessly pinned under them and was being pawed by two others whose tails were wagging wildly. The tangle of pups rolled onto the ice which gave way. They all began to splash and squeal in the shallow water. Alphie waded in and pulled them to shore.

Ripples rolled across the pond, distorting the dark feathered reflection of the raptor that circled above. Attracted by the distress calls of the pups, the golden eagle soared in great circles over Druid Pond. She studied the scene below. Bright sunlight was now on the pond where newly formed wisps of vapor moved above the water like spirits. On shore, every branch and blade of grass had its own diamond, a frozen bead of water that turned sunlight into silver jewels. All eight pups were playing further and further from their babysitter who stood close to the pond. He watched the meadow and forest for danger.

Alphie saw the bird's reflection before he saw the bird. It was sliding down the sky toward the pups, its dark brown wings wide and talons forward. The eagle intended to snatch a pup and fly away. Air rushed over the wings causing an *audible* flutter, a sound that Alphie knew, a sound that pushed him into action. He bolted toward the pups and leapt into the air stretching out full length to intercept the winged predator. Unfortunately, he missed and splashed into the water. The bird wavered in its flight long enough for the pups to take cover behind a rotted log. The eagle swooped over them, then turned upward and climbed into the sky. Alphie ran toward the pups as the eagle turned down into a second dive. From this new direction, the pups were fully exposed. The eagle tucked her wings a little to increase her speed. Alphie became a blur running toward the whining pups. He leapt into the path of the descending bird, and they collided with such force that Alphie came away with a mouthful of feathers, and the angry bird screeched and flapped its dark wings until it disappeared over the tree tops. Alphie stood over the pups with feathers stuck to his lips.

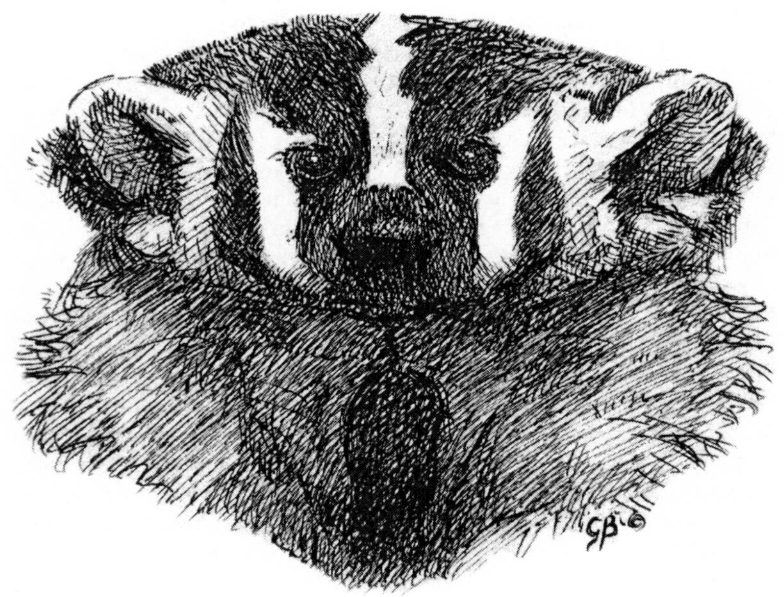

WOLF
42F
... ON PATROL
2006

Fold when
leg back
Ribcage shoots
up to pelvis
Tibia
1/2 Femur
Jaw Drop
wide
@ elbows
Rt Hind

WOLF
21M
GBuman

Chapter Six

Gradually, as days turned into weeks, the Lamar Valley became awash in green with hints of color. Flowers flourished and grasses grew tall. The sage brush stretched its stiff, gray-green arms to support meadow larks and Uinta ground squirrels. Balsamroot began to bloom like clusters of yellow sunlight. Goatsbeard seeded up like giant dandelions. Leopard lilies began to open, and the flaming leaves of common Indian paintbrush added their yellow, orange, red, and pink to nature's *palette*.

The Lamar Pack pups had doubled in size. One black was almost twenty pounds, while the others were slightly smaller. They were spending more and more time outside the crowded den. They still nursed, but were eating more regurgitated food. Mother Wolf and Pearly were often away on hunts with the pack. Now that Grandfather was missing, Alphie got to stay behind more to help with the pups, a duty he loved.

One day in late June, there was a stirring around both dens. Papa Wolf had left with most of the pack for a hunt near Trout Lake. Even though Mother Wolf and Pearly remained, they had asked Alphie to stay as well. Alphie sensed that something was about to happen. All eight pups were running in a big circle that included a moss covered log, a castle of rocks, and a tunnel made by boulders leaning against each other. The pups had to squeeze through the tunnel now that they had grown so much. They snapped at one another, rolled around on the ground, and made sudden leaps into the air trying to capture imaginary prey.

Alphie joined in the fun. He pinned pups with his large paws. He romped beside them as they ran their course over and over. He could not fit through the tunnel but, instead, ran around the rock and startled the pups when they emerged from the dark hole.

After some time Alphie could see that Mother Wolf and Pearly were pacing back and forth. "Is something wrong?" he asked.

"No, Alphie," said Mother Wolf. "It's just that we're leaving today."

"To hunt?" he asked.

"No. We are all leaving. It's time to move the pups to the rendezvous. They've outgrown the den. I think they're strong enough to make the Crossing. Will you help?"

Alphie asked, "What should I do?"

Pearly said, "Mother and I will lead the pups. We would like you to follow to make sure none get lost or left behind. Grandfather wanted to do this with us, but he's not here."

"If we leave, how will he find us?" Alphie seemed a little panicked.

Mother Wolf said, "Puppies leave a strong scent trail. Grandfather will be able to find us. Don't worry about him. Stay focused on the pups. They may think we are just going for a walk, but this time we won't be coming back."

After Mother Wolf barked at the *rambunctious* pups, they formed a ragged line and followed her and Pearly. Alphie checked the den, the tunnel, and a half dozen other hiding places before he was satisfied that no pups were left behind. Leaving the den stirred anxious memories of his own departure from there a year ago. The bonds to his birth place were strong and not easily broken. Moving to a new place is never easy. Recalling his own Crossing, Alphie remembered that by the time Mother Wolf had dragged him across the rushing water of Soda Butte Creek, it was discovered that Yarrow and Lupine were missing. Pearly, then just a yearling, ran up and down the creek certain that the pups had been swept away and drowned. However, Papa Wolf discovered their scent trail and followed it all the way back to the den where he found them asleep. It took many hours, Alphie recalled, to convince the frightened females to cross.

Now Alphie realized the full weight of his responsibilities. He rushed down the slope through the den forest. The pups were just passing the old teepee poles, sagging against the pines, when Alphie caught up. The pups took turns breaking from the line to investigate a stick, climb a stump, or attack a large black beetle stumbling along in the dirt. One black pup drifted quite far from the group. She found a wandering garter snake that looked like a piece of pale brownish-green rope slithering through the grass near a trickle of water. The small wolf tentatively placed her paw on the thin serpent which immediately lunged at her with fangs exposed. The startled pup jumped back, then, whimpering, quickly rejoined the others.

The afternoon sun had caused wild blue flax to open their petals. Held by slender stalks, they bowed in the slight breeze to the wolves passing among them. The air was a perfume of flax and sage. Smell is an invisible key that unlocks memories. It was *deja vu* for Alphie; he was a pup again. He ran in great circles through the wide meadow of blue flowers. He vaulted over sage bushes and pups. The pups became excited, as well, and soon were running in all directions below the blue sky and through the blue flowers.

The one thing that had no odor was the newborn elk calf hiding in nearby sage. Its mother had licked it clean and told it to stay. The calf's coat was the same color as the brown dust which surrounded it. The cow ran off trying to lure the wolves away from her calf. However, the wolves not only did not notice her, they ran right past the bedded calf. The calf watched a parade of wolf legs rush by.

Mother wolf and Pearly were waiting patiently by Soda Butte Creek. Mother Wolf finally gave a short bark. The pups ran to her and stared wide-eyed at the rushing water. Even though the stream was only a few dozen yards wide at this crossing place, the water was deep and fast. Its single note was like a hard wind blowing through trees. The pups whined their nervousness. Mother Wolf spoke loudly over the noise of the water, "Don't worry. If we enter here, it will carry us to that sandbar on the far side near the bend. Keep swimming toward the other side and you'll be fine. Watch me and Pearly; then you follow."

Mother Wolf waded into the creek with her long legs but was soon in swift water up to her neck. Facing the far side she pawed at the water as she was being carried downstream. Pearly entered the water, as well, and followed Mother Wolf to the sandbar fifty feet from the pups. Both mothers shook off water, then signaled the pups to follow.

The pups refused to cross. They paced along the bank and whimpered their fear. Alphie waded into the water to show that there was no danger. Pearly's gray pup turned north and headed back toward the den. Alphie splashed out of the water and headed her off. He clamped his jaws over the back of the little wolf and let out a mild growl. The pup rejoined the others.

Mother Wolf's black pup, the biggest of the pups, was the first to enter the stream. The frigid water spun him around so that he was facing downstream, but his frantic strokes pulled him closer to the far shore where, bobbing like a cork, he was caught by Mother Wolf and dragged onto the sandbar. The little thing shook off water and scampered up the bank where he followed Pearly into the field. The pair bedded. Pearly licked the wet pup who squirmed between her paws.

Two more pups braved the racing current and were swept down toward Mother Wolf. She was able to intercept both pups and nudge them into shallow water where they shook and ran off to Pearly. And so it went with the next two pups. Alphie could hear their hysterical cries as they swam for their lives. Mother Wolf was able to get both pups on their feet and off to Pearly.

Five had crossed, three to go. The black and two grays that remained had lost their focus and began to play. One pup had picked up a mossy green stone which the other two were trying to get from him. Alphie interrupted the game and managed to get all three into the water. They squealed and sputtered as they were washed downstream. Alphie ran next to them on shore. He raced ahead, then back as they frantically pawed the icy water. Mother Wolf was able to get the black and one of the grays up on shore. The other pup, Pearly's gray, pawed in the wrong direction and floated close to the north bank of the stream where the water was deep and swift. While Mother Wolf was busy with the other two pups, the tiny gray was swept downstream around the bend.

Alphie saw her disappear under water. He sprinted along the bank. By the time he got around the bend, he could see the small pup tumbling in the rapids, head up, then feet, then tail. Alphie scrambled to the end of the rapids just in time to see her slip under the surface of the deep pool. Without hesitation the black yearling dove into the dark, swirling water. The gray pup popped up like a piece of driftwood. He allowed the current to hold the shivering gray against his side as he swam to the far bank.

Alphie picked the pup up by the scruff of its neck and carried it to a grassy spot between two old cottonwood trees. The pup lay on its side and allowed Alphie to lick it. Then she stood and shook off.

Alphie said, "That was a scary ride! Grandfather would call it the nightmare of every pup. We better catch up with the others." The big black yearling trotted off with the little gray close behind. One crossing done, one to go.

Chapter Seven

Pearly was bedded on a high bank on the west side of the Lamar River, which curved through a grove of cottonwoods. The circumferences of two of the trees had been scarred by beavers. Pearly watched as Mother Wolf and Alphie helped each pup make the crossing in wild water. She could hear the shrill cries of the little ones over the sustained whoosh of the river. As each pup made the small beach on the other side, it would climb the steep bank and rub against Pearly's white fur.

Mother Wolf and Alphie stayed closer to each pup because the Lamar was wider and faster than Soda Butte had been. Two of the pups had to be carried across, and there were anxious moments for some of the others. All eight finally made it and swarmed over the adults in their wet joy. Pearly's gray pup, who had already turned back toward the den once, tried to go back again. The den was her safe zone, a place of family smells and warm hiding places. The little pup was about to leap back into the rushing water when Mother Wolf picked her up and carried her back to where the others were playing.

The three adults groomed the pups as they played. In time, they resumed their *trek* west across the sage flats toward Chalcedony Creek and the rendezvous site. Spread out down the valley was a large bison herd, mostly cows and calves with a few young bulls. Some of the calves born late in the birthing season still had thick, reddish fur. They ran around their mothers and butted one another. The cows, several hundred in number, were grazing their way east very slowly. The only path to the rendezvous was through the herd.

Alphie took the lead. As he moved into the herd at a slow pace, the bison moved aside. The cows moved their calves away from the dark predator. Most calves remained behind a wall of very large mothers. The cows could tell by the way Alphie moved that he was not hunting. One young bull raised his tail to show his agitation, but retreated quickly when Alphie drew near.

Mother Wolf followed Alphie, the pups followed her, and Pearly followed them. The large black pup broke from the line and confronted a bison calf. Out of curiosity the calf lowered his head and sniffed the pup. For a moment they were nose to nose until the calf's mother snorted, sending the pup scrambling back to the line. Pearly's little gray pup was terrified of the huge beasts and all of their grumpy noises. She walked the whole way through the herd protected by her mother's long legs.

Beyond the bison they found the eroded area, an open pit with small gullies carved by wind and water. The pups raced around playing hide-n-seek and tackling one another. One low spot contained water, where they splashed and drank. Further on, where sage gave way to grass, they found a low mound of bare dirt, a great place to rest or play. Fortunately for the three adults, the pups chose to rest. One by one they snuggled into the dust of the mound, some with feet in the air, some on their sides looking as if they had just dropped from the sky. Behind them were the three low foothills, each as high as a bull bison's back, where last fall Alphie had watched his pack *evict* the invading Garnet Peak Pack. Beyond the foothills, forest covered the north wall of Specimen Ridge. The lower forest, the foothills, the mound, and the eroded area were all part of the rendezvous site, the puppies' new home.

Chapter Eight

The sun was a shimmering red wafer on the western horizon when the puppies woke up. The cloud bank that stretched north and south was magenta, with light pink clouds flaring up into the darkening sky. The pups stretched and yawned in the red twilight, the *crepuscular* time of day when so many animals become active. Several of the pups could see wolves approaching from the direction of the river. They began to bark, which set off the others. Two of the pups leapt on Mother Wolf, Pearly, and Alphie. Alphie jumped up and saw the wolves. He howled a warning.

Mother Wolf said, "Wait, Alphie. That might be Papa returning with the others. Let them get closer."

It was when the incoming wolves approached the eroded area that Alphie recognized Papa Wolf. He tucked his tail as he ran out to greet the returning hunters. The two mothers and the pups rushed out, as well. In the dusty gullies there was a huge reunion. The wolves jumped on one another and whined their joy. Tails wagged and bodies rubbed against each other. The pups made their needs known by licking the faces of the hunters. Each one regurgitated several times. The pups and their babysitters ate eagerly.

Finally, Alphie said to Papa, "Did you see Grandfather?"

Papa replied quietly, "Yes we did, Alphie. He was near the cliffs above Trout Lake. We gave him a slab of elk meat. I think that it was a good sign that he ate. But you should know, Alphie, that he still hurts inside where the bull kicked him. It's more difficult for an older wolf to recover from such an injury. If he heals, Grandfather will return to us. Until then, he needs to rest."

"I'll go see him right now!" Alphie blurted out.

"Not quite so fast," said Papa. "After we have a rest, Pearly and Mother will return with us to the carcass way up Pebble Creek. It will be midday before we get back. Because you're the biggest of the yearlings, you'll protect the pups while we are gone. You can go to Grandfather when we return."

Alphie looked at the ground and said, "Yes, Papa. I'll wait until then."

Darkness seeped into the valley. Alphie showed the pups more of their new home. He led them over the foothills and showed them the large, flat rock in the woods where he used to play tag with his brothers and sisters. He showed them the secret cave where he hid from the bear and the lion, where he first met Grandfather. They all crowded in the cave and Alphie told them story after story about their great grandfather. Then he said to them, "This is where you hide when trouble shows itself."

Eventually, they all returned to the foothills where the rest of the pack had bedded. This was the first night the pups had not slept in a den. They were restless and stirred at the sound the wind made combing through grass, sage, and woods. Small heads rose every time the valley lit up from lightning so far away that the thunder could not be heard. The pups snuggled closer to the sleeping adults as the warm air cooled and a light rain began to fall.

Come first light when the pups awoke, they were surprised to discover that except for Alphie the pack was gone. Alphie comforted them with grooming licks and playful swats with his paws. He allowed the pups to crawl onto him and tug at his dark fur. Finally, he led them to the dirt mound near the sage. He bedded nearby while they chased each other, attacked sage bushes, and used an old piece of hide for tug-o-war.

Even though Alphie was bedded, he remained *vigilant*, always looking for possible danger. The sky was no longer a threat because the pups were too big now to be carried off by an eagle. Alphie knew, though, that trouble could come from any direction. Every few minutes, he would stand to get a longer view in both directions, investigate a sound, or read an odor that floated on the breeze.

It was that attentiveness that allowed Alphie to feel the bison charging from the west before he heard or saw them. Even the pups stopped their games when they felt the ground shake. Alphie barked, sounding the alarm. The pups scrambled over the Middle Foothill to the secret cave. Alphie watched from the woods as a large herd of bison cows and calves stampeded through the rendezvous site. The reddish calves ran in the middle of the herd where they would be protected from whatever it was that had spooked them. The hooves of the large animals kicked up clods of mud. Several had their ropey tails straight up indicating that they were angry about something. Alphie could hear the bison muttering in deep voices as they thundered across sage covered meadows.

The bison herd, a hundred strong, slowed as it approached the Lamar River. Cows crossed downstream from their calves in order to guide them through the swift water. Once across, they hurried into the open fields along the base of Mount Norris. There they quieted themselves and grazed. Some of the calves nudged their mothers and began to nurse. For a long moment, a pronghorn stood by the river looking west for the trouble, but, seeing nothing, resumed grazing.

When the coast was clear, the pups followed Alphie out of the woods. It appeared as though the danger was over. Part of being wild involved knowing that your life depended on being able to detect a sudden threat before it detected you. The pups had just had another lesson about survival that they would not forget. For now they played among some aspen trees that grew along the edge of the forest, but school was not over for the day.

Alphie stood guard on the Middle Foothill. He was looking east toward the cluster of cottonwood trees where the bison had disappeared. An odor on the wind caused him to turn to the west. Rounding the Western Foothill, not far from him, was the reason for the bison stampede: a sow grizzly and her coy. The cub of the year, about the size of a wolf pup, followed close behind its mother. The sow, three times the size of Alphie, moved slowly along the base of the foothill. She was a light, silvery bear with a dark brown scarf of fur about her neck. The cub was a copy of its mother. The sow, however, had an enormous hump near her shoulders, which advertised her terrible strength.

Alphie gave out a warning bark howl that sent the pups scurrying back to the cave. The sow instantly stood up on her hind legs to search for the source of the noise. The cub did the same. They stood with their front paws hanging at their sides. Alphie remembered what Grandfather had said, that a bear alone is dangerous, but one with a cub is double danger. "If she thinks her cub is threatened, she will fight to the death," he had said.

Alphie had little ones to protect, too, so he did not flinch or back away. If she discovered the pups, it would be very bad. Alphie charged off the high ground like a black streak heading directly at the bear and cub. The cub disappeared behind its mother. The sow dropped down on all fours and charged the yearling. Alphie *veered* off at the last minute and headed for the mound. The sow chased after him, with the cub close on her heals. The cub was bawling, the sow was growling and huffing, and Alphie was barking and snarling. On the mound Alphie turned around and snarled again at the bear. She stopped suddenly which caused the cub to crash into her. Alphie charged her with his teeth bared and his tail high.

Surprised at his sudden boldness, the grizzly ran a short distance away making sure that her cub was close by. The young wolf continued his rush until she stood up again and swatted at him with one of her great paws. Alphie remembered Grandfather pointing at an aspen tree trunk with four parallel scars from a grizzly paw. His casual comment that he never wanted to look like that scarred trunk made Alphie extra careful now. He jumped clear and began circling the bear. She turned, too, keeping herself between the wolf and her cub.

Alphie dashed around the sow, but she spun to face him. She now had her cub under her. She bluff charged the yearling, then hurried back to her exposed cub. Alphie circled and circled, and then, when he got behind the bear, he struck. He leapt in close and bit the sow on her rump, then jumped back out of reach. The sow exploded with a great roar, her long muscles clenched under her fur. She charged. Alphie ran into the tall sage, effectively leading the bear further and further from the pups. The bear had to keep checking to see that her cub was next to her. Each time she looked back to find the black wolf, he was gone. Then Alphie would surprise her from behind with another bite, after which he would disappear further into the sage.

Finally Alphie made a big circle back to the Middle Foothill. From there he could see the sow still searching for him. He could mostly see her back, except when she spun around trying to avoid being surprised with another bite. As she moved further off toward the river, she kept ushering her cub ahead of her. Alphie couldn't see the cub, but saw the sage move each time it bumped against the brush. He whispered aloud, "Grandfather, you would have loved this."

The yearling wolf watched the sow and cub until he was satisfied that they would not return. He lifted his head high and howled his victory, "Ahooohoooohooooo." When the pups did not come out of the woods, he trotted up to the secret cave. All eight pups were packed into the small shelter, a wad of wolves with a leg sticking out here, there a tail, a few pairs of closed eyes, an assortment of ears, some parts black, some the color of dried grass. They were all sound asleep. Alphie curled up next to them and closed his eyes.

Chapter Nine

Alphie was in the middle of a dream in which he and Grandfather had treed a mountain lion that had attempted to take over their hard won carcass, when a real howl from across the valley woke him. The puppies were already stirring. The light along the river was red from the flaming sunset. The pups followed Alphie out to the Middle Foothill where they joined him in his howl response. Their high pitched voices were like sirens compared to Alphie's long bass notes. "Ahooohooooohoooo" they called across the valley.

Soon Mother Wolf and Papa appeared in the eroded area with a half dozen other pack members strung out in a line that stretched back to the river. They were trotting with full bellies toward the rendezvous. The pups charged off the low hill and rushed the alphas. They jumped up on both of them, licked their faces, and squealed their hunger. Simultaneously, the alphas lowered their heads and regurgitated a warm meal. The pups ate as if they were in a competition. Then they raced to the other wolves as they arrived and repeated their begging until their hunger was satisfied.

Alphie ate leftovers where he could find them. Mostly, though, he wanted news about Grandfather. Mother Wolf said, "I'm sorry, Alphie. We didn't see him. I was sure he would be at the carcass. There's plenty for him to eat, and eagles and ravens in every tree to let him know where to look. But he was nowhere to be seen."

Papa Wolf bedded, then said, "I don't know if he is still at Trout Lake. We took some elk meat there on our way back, but there was a bear with a cub near the lake. She was in a foul mood so we circled around her to avoid trouble."

"I know that bear," Alphie said.

Papa continued, "We cached the meat near the ancient tree just below the lake. If that sow hasn't dug it up, you might take it with you in case you find Grandfather. You should go now and look for him. Remember, Alphie, he's an old, injured wolf and may have wandered off to be with the ancestors. You go now. If you do find him, lead him home."

The red light had bled out of the sky as the valley rolled away from the sun, and darker clouds drifted over Junction Butte turning the air gray. Alphie trotted east. He swam the Lamar River, but stayed south of Soda Butte Creek, choosing to follow a trail below the high cliffs of Mount Norris. He trotted past a burned out snag, a tall tree stump sculpture carved by fire back in '88. South of Soda Butte Cone, a small volcano-shaped deposit built up around a hot spring that was the source of the stink water that perfumed the air, Alphie came upon some coyote commotion. It seems that a coyote stranger had wandered too close to an occupied coyote den, and the angry alphas had attacked the trespasser. They had him trapped against a fallen tree. As the young wolf watched, the cornered coyote tucked his thick tail, hunched up his back, curled into a kind of 'u' shape, and, with head low and teeth exposed, he snarled and hissed at the pair who harassed him. In this angry posture, he inched his way toward the barking alphas. They retreated, at first, then presented the same posture to the intruder who backed off. All three coyotes paused in their altercation long enough to watch the black wolf trot past. Once clear of the scene, Alphie could hear them resume their territorial *feud.*

Alphie continued east in the dim light, working his way along a slope thick with aspen. The black wolf moving among the pale barked tree trunks looked like a painting in motion. The new aspen leaves vibrated in the strengthening breeze. The first flashes of lightning came from the west, lighting the whole valley for an instant as if it were midday. The sudden daylight was followed by thunder, booming up the valley and ricocheting off the high cliffs. The boulders of sound rolled over Alphie and settled in the steeper valleys upstream near Thunderer and Barronette Peak.

Alphie trotted on. He could move at this pace all day, if it was necessary. As he moved, his mind raced, a film loop of worry about Grandfather taking his last breaths alone. The memory of the yearling wolf was stirred, as well, with snapshots of the many times Grandfather had rescued him, had comforted him, had made him laugh. Alphie knew now that the seed of confidence that grew in him every day had been planted there by that old wolf, who now was alone out in the dark. The young wolf worried about the approaching storm. He worried about how strong the wind was and how icy cold the rain would be for Grandfather. With each flash of thought, Alphie quickened his pace until he was in a full run, a shadow running among shadows.

Lightning flashed and thunder rolled across the valley. Just shy of Round Prairie, Alphie turned north. He flew over fallen trees, leapt right or left to avoid stiff branches, and crashed through thick bushes. Soda Butte Creek was narrow and fast where he crossed. He dashed up a steep trail that paralleled the outlet creek for Trout Lake. Hail began to fall like bullets shredding flowers and leaves. Soon the hail turned to rain, a downpour the young wolf ignored.

Down hill from the lake was the old tree he was seeking. The Douglas Fir had stood here for centuries. As it often did in storms, the tree danced while wind whistled through its branches. Rivulets of rain water coursed down the dark, coarse bark. The tree's trunk was a thick column that seemed to hold up the sky. Alphie remembered that Grandfather had once told him that you have to admire the patience of this old tree. He sniffed around the base of the tree searching for the slab of meat that Papa had cached there. Unfortunately, when he located the spot, the meat was gone. Not even this hard rain could wash away the smell of bear. Grandfather would not eat tonight.

Undeterred, Alphie moved on up the trail. The lightning intensified, as did the thunder and rain. Multiple flashes of lightning struck near Trout Lake. The surface reflected the white light upward to *illuminate* the heavens, where clouds tumbled and swirled like a boiling river. Thunder crashed against the cliffs up the slope above the lake. Even the echo shook the ground. Alphie hesitated long enough to howl. "Ahooohooohooooo," he called into the darkness. His howl was mournful and filled with all of the worried emotions at play in his heart. There was no reply. "Grandfather!" he cried. No response. His voice was absorbed by the storm. He shook water from his coat and moved along the east side of the lake. At the inlet, he howled and called again. Still no answer. He moved to the east and stood on a high ridge overlooking Buck Lake, a pond where river otters were known to play. Alphie howled and called. Nothing. He turned north again and climbed to tiny Shrimp Lake, a small pond near the cliffs. No answer there either.

Where the lower cliff rock formed an overhanging shelf, Alphie found Grandfather's scent in the dry *duff*. The odor was faint where pine needles and grass had been compressed into a bed. "Grandfather,"

Alphie whispered. Thunder drowned out his small voice. Grandfather was gone. The old smell was slightly stronger as Alphie sniffed along the base of the cliff. Then Alphie looked out into the wet darkness. Rain was falling, wind was howling, lightning and thunder were taking turns in their violent conversation. Amidst all that chaos, Alphie was remembering.

The yearling wolf almost smiled. "Mountain Lion Cave," he said aloud. "That's where you've gone!" He bolted into the darkness. He sprinted around Shrimp Lake and across exposed rock along the shore of Buck Lake. As he ran east through thick forest, his head was full of memories. In the fall and then again in winter, Grandfather had showed Alphie his secret place in Pebble Creek Canyon. In winter, they had to chase a big cat out of the cave. Grandfather had said, "Too bad for lion that we both have the same secret cave." The cave was deep and comfortable, dry even during the high water of spring, Grandfather had told the young wolf. In winter the creek flowed under deep snow and ice by the mouth of the cave. Alphie loved to feel it move beneath his feet and listen to its gurgling voice under the clear, windblown glass of the ice.

Alphie followed an elk trail down the hillside to a flat meadow where Pebble Creek gushed out of the canyon. His pace slowed to a trot as he entered the narrow passageway heading upstream. The rock face walls on either side were close together and glistened with each flash of lightning. The storm front had moved further east so that the thunder was more distant and a little muffled in the wet canyon, more like the memory of the sound than the sound itself. Pines and fir trees hung out over the canyon walls, their roots holding onto rock like the talons of ancient raptors.

Chapter Ten

The canyon was like a crack in the earth. It curved right, then left. Alphie's eyes were made for darkness and they enabled him to chose his footing well as he jumped from boulder to boulder. He walked beneath the gaze of the Spirit of Pebble Creek, deep impressions in the rock wall that appeared to be a face, maybe Native American, Crow perhaps, whose eyes watched all who passed there.

Alphie stopped near the cave entrance. He wasn't close enough to see inside. Across the stream from the entrance was a lodgepole pine that had tipped over in the canyon years ago and had come to rest at a low angle above the broken rock floor. The yearling was about to call out for Grandfather when a snake-like movement caught his eye. A stutter of lightening revealed the details of the mountain lion pressed against the tree trunk, its tail slowly moving in the dark air. She turned her gaze away from the cave and looked straight at Alphie, her intense eyes set in a small, round face.

Several times Grandfather had told Alphie that going up against a large cat alone was not a good idea. "They are powerful fighters, " he had said. "They can shred a wolf even if it has the cat by the neck. Some of our ancestors became ancestors at the claws and jaws of big cats." Alphie also remembered Grandfather saying, "If a fight can't be avoided, be the first to charge and make a lot of noise. The big cats have an *inferiority complex* and are actually scaredy cats. If you growl loud enough, they'll run for the hills!"

In this case in Pebble Creek Canyon, a fight could not be avoided. Alphie charged the large cat. His primitive growl came from deep in his throat and was *amplified* by the slick canyon walls. He bared his teeth and snapped at the big cat. The cat yowled its surprise and ran the length of the fallen tree. When the cat ran out of tree, she leapt onto a boulder and bounded upstream out of sight. Alphie watched her go.

He turned toward the cave. Thunder was a soft, distant drum. The rain had eased. Some night sounds crept into the canyon: boreal chorus frogs, a few crickets, a great horned owl. Appearing like a piece of moon each time the lightening flickered, Grandfather, with his almost white fur, lay on his side deep in the cave. The cave floor was a heap of broken stone chiseled from the canyon walls by thousands of years of ice.

Alphie went to Grandfather. He was thin; his coat was matted with mud and prickly thistles. But he was breathing. His silver chest rose and fell. Alphie could see now that the old wolf's light fur made the crescent moon on his chest disappear. "Grandfather," he whispered. "Grandfather, it's me, Alphie."

The old wolf lifted his head and then lowered it again. Alphie began to groom him. He licked his fur clean of mud. He nibbled gently with his teeth to clean the caked on dirt. Alphie bit loose those thistles that had tangled themselves in Grandfather's tail and in the rough fur around his neck.

"Grandfather," Alphie said, "the pack made a kill not far from here. I'll get you something to eat. I'll be back in no time."

Without raising his head, Grandfather said, "Wait, Alphie. Don't go. Stay with me. Everything will be okay. Lie right here so you can hear me."

The old wolf's voice was so soft, so weak that Alphie bedded close to him, their heads almost touching. Alphie was so excited that he began by telling Grandfather all about the Crossing and the bison stampede and the grizzly sow with the cub. Then Alphie realized that he was talking when the old wolf wanted to speak.

Finally Grandfather whispered, "You know, Alphie, you are a brave wolf. You have proven your courage already and you're just a yearling. Very amazing wolf, that is what you are. When the pack is recalling its victories, some of the praise songs will be sung for you."

The old wolf coughed, breathed rapidly for a moment, and then continued, "I admire courage, but my own grandfather had other kinds of heroes. They were the teachers and storytellers among us. I admire them, too. And because you are both of those, I admire you. You have already been teaching the pups how to find their place in the pack. Soon you will teach them to hunt, to read an elk, how to survive in this wild place, how to respect family, and how to laugh. I hope you always keep the puppy in you alive. It's not important to have a long life; it's important to have an interesting life. Stirring up some fun every day will help. And, Alphie, I know your heart is filling with stories to tell. You already have all the ones I've told you. But, most important, you now have your own stories with many more to come. I just wanted you to know why I admire you so much."

"Grandfather," Alphie said quietly, "you're my hero, too."

The yearling put his paw on Grandfather's shoulder. He realized that the old wolf was shivering. Alphie moved in closer and leaned against Grandfather in an attempt to share his warmth. He could still feel the trembling. He lay in the dark cave watching the very faint flickers of lightning dance on the rushing water of the creek. He could still hear the thunder booming softly in the distance. For a while the yearling black wolf swam in the memories he shared with the old wolf next to him. Images bloomed and faded.

After a time Grandfather whispered, "Would you tell me a story, Alphie?"

The yearling took a moment to arrange all the story details in his head in the proper order. Then he said quietly, "Once upon a time there was a little black wolf who woke up one day to find his family gone..." Alphie rambled on about all the adventures the little wolf pup had had with his grandfather. The quiet rhythm of the yearling's voice was a comfort to the old wolf. At some point, deep in the middle of all of those adventures, when a coyote was being tricked or a grizzly outsmarted, Grandfather's shivering ceased.

Hours later the thin gray light of morning seeped into Pebble Creek Canyon where it was washed in the rushing sound and churning mist of the creek. Alphie stretched and yawned. Slowly he sat up in the half dark cave and listened to water tumbling over rock. He turned to Grandfather and nudged him with his nose. Grandfather did not move. Alphie pushed him with his paw. No response. Alphie whined as he sniffed the old wolf. Then he turned away.

At the entrance of the cave, the yearling howled long and low, a mourning song that carried in its notes all the hurt of a loved one lost. The sorrowful howl braided itself among the natural notes of the rushing creek and floated downstream toward the meadows of Round Prairie. As he howled, Alphie gradually became aware, in some wolf way, that during this first year of his life, Grandfather's courage, survival skills, loyalty to family, and love of laughter had become a part of him. Grandfather's words would be Alphie's guide through the wild landscape of life. Grandfather's ways would be Alphie's ways.

The young wolf moved out of the canyon and into the open meadows through which Soda Butte Creek flowed. He was stopped along the creek bank by wolf howls coming from the west. The voices were faint but familiar. Alphie began to trot downstream, often looking back to see the shadow of the old wolf match his pace step for step. The yearling broke into a run brushing by sage, leaping over drift logs, crossing gulleys, and splashing through shallow water with the spirit of the old wolf right on his heels. Mountain blue birds and a bison watched him pass. He ran toward the distant rendezvous; he ran toward his pack; he ran toward the playful pups. Alphie ran toward the same prey that Grandfather pursued all of his days; he ran toward the wild life of Lamar Valley.

Glossary

absorbing: drawn into, like water into a sponge

alluvial fan: a triangular formation of land where a stream has deposited soil

alpha sign: Wolves communicate a lot through body language. The leader of a pack will keep his tail . raised high to let others know that he is the top wolf in the pack. When a wolf tucks his tail between his legs, he is saying to others that he is subordinate (lower in rank) and frightened. It would be interesting to research other ways wolves communicate with each other within the pack and outside the pack.

alphas: the leaders of the pack, a male and female wolf

ambush: a surprise attack

amplified: made louder

ancestral: having to do with ancestors, the preceding generations

ancient: very old

anxiety: a feeling of worry, nervousness

audible: able to be heard

avalanche: Usually an avalanche occurs when snow or soil and rock break loose from a mountain and rush down the slope to the valley. In this story, thunder crashes down the mountainside like an "avalanche of sound".

averted: looking to one side or at the ground; not making eye contact

boggy: wet, muddy ground (If you walked in a boggy area, you would most likely sink in and risk losing a sneaker or a boot.)

bonds: ties, feelings for one another

bough: branch

cached: Many animals and birds hide food for later use. Wolves, for example, often bury chunks of meat, which they intend to dig up later for another meal.

cacophony: a harsh mixture of sounds
canids: any mammal of the dog family (In Yellowstone, if we see a wolf, a coyote, and a fox on the same day, we say that we had "a three dog day", each of which is a canid.)
catapulted: thrown into the air

Chalcedony Creek: (kal,sed',nee) The Creek is named after a type of quartz mineral found in the area. Many of the place names in Yellowstone are taken from minerals and rocks found nearby.

chaos: disorder and confusion

coarse: rough in texture

confluence: where two rivers meet or where a creek joins a river

consequences: results of an action

coy: cub of the year (c. o. y.)

crepuscular: twilight (first light of morning; last light of day)

Crossing: When wolf pups are too big for the den, about three months old, they are led to a rendezvous site. For wolves denning near Druid Peak, the trip to the rendezvous included crossing Soda Butte Creek and the Lamar River. The Crossing was always dangerous because of high, fast water.

deja vu: the feeling that one has already had this experience

delicacies: pleasing taste

deterred: discouraged

Disappearance: When Grandfather talks about the Disappearance, he means that time in the recent past during which wolves were exterminated (killed) in most of America by human beings. In 1995, wolves from Canada were reintroduced to Yellowstone and several neighboring states. Scientists discovered that wolves were a critical part of the environment, one of the main links in the food chain. Without the wolf, many plants, animals, and birds suffered.

disgruntled: upset

distress: extreme anxiety; nervousness

dominant: taking the part of the leader, boss wolf, top dog

duff: decaying plant matter covering the ground

earnest: with a serious attitude

eerily: unearthly, frightening

emerged: came out of

enthusiasm: excitement

eroded: Flowing water washes away earth (erosion), creating deep ditches (gullies).

evict: chase out

excavated: dug up

fairyslipper: a pink orchid flower shaped like a slipper found in shaded places in June

feud: a long disagreement that may involve some fighting

fossils: The remains or impressions of a prehistoric organism preserved as a mold or cast in rock

formidable: inspiring respect by being impressively large

gait: manner of walking

geysers: hot springs that boil over, sending water and steam into the air

Great Fire: In 1988, thirty-six percent of Yellowstone burned. That is 793,880 acres. An additional 500,000 acres burned outside the Park boundaries. Of the fifty-one separate fires, nine were caused by man, forty-two were caused by lightning. (Source: Yellowstone Resource and Issues, 2007)

grim: gruesome, harsh, unpleasant

harebells: The roundleaf harebell has purple, bell shaped flowers that hang down from a tall stem.

harem: a small group of cow elk, with which a single bull hopes to mate during the fall breeding season

horizontal: on the same line as the horizon, left to right rather than up and down (vertical)

illuminate: cast light upon

inferiority complex: a feeling of not being as good as others

interlopers: wolves that have come into an area where they are not wanted

intimidate: frighten

intruders: wolves that have entered the Lamar Pack territory with the intent of taking it over

jawed: Often adult wolves discipline pups by pinning them to the ground with their jaws. They do not bite down, but just hold them firmly. Wolves also jaw each other as a friendly gesture to show affection.

kestrel: An American Kestrel is also known as a Sparrow Hawk. The size of a blue jay, this small raptor (bird of prey) eats small birds, insects, and rodents. Unlike larger falcons, the kestrel catches its prey on the ground, rather than in the air.

laden: weighed down

malnourished: the result of having a poor diet

mane: You are familiar with the mane on a horse, the long hair along the back of its neck. In this story, the word is used to describe the longer fur on the front half of the bull bison.

marmot: The yellow-bellied marmot, a cousin of the eastern groundhog, is a large rodent living in the mountains of the west. They like the high elevations. The Lamar Valley, where this story is set, is about 6500 feet above sea level.

maze: A complex network of paths and dead ends through which Alphie and Grandfather must find their way

meager: lacking in quality or quantity

melancholy: sad

millennia: thousands of years

morsels: small pieces of food

nostrils: nose openings

nuisance: annoyance, bothersome

ominously: suggesting something bad may happen

palette: a range of colors used by an artist

Petrified Forest: a group of trees turned to stone as a result of ancient volcanic activity

plateau: a high, flat landscape

pounce: leap upon

predicament: a difficult situation
pulverizing: crushing

pursuing: chasing
rambunctious: unruly

raptors: birds of prey (hawks, eagles, owls)

refuge: condition of being safe; protected from danger

regurgitation: vomiting, throwing up

rendezvous: (ran'da,voo) Once wolf pups outgrow the den and are done nursing, the adults move them to an open area with some shade and water. The pups remain near this spot with one or more adult babysitter wolves while the other adults hunt. When elk move into the high country during late summer, wolves may well move their pups to a new high country rendezvous.

rousing: awakening

rubbed out: killed

sediment: soil

sentries: guards looking for danger

serenade: love song

sheath: a close-fitting cover

siblings: brothers & sisters

simultaneously: at the same time

snipe: a long billed, brownish shorebird

snowmelt: In the high mountains, heavy snow piles up all winter. In the spring, the snow begins to melt and the water runs into the valley, causing the creeks and rivers to rise rapidly. Sometimes the water current is so swift, it can sweep a bison calf downstream. Fast water created by snowmelt in the mountains is very dangerous for small wolf puppies trying to cross streams to get to their rendezvous sites.

solitary: alone

stamina: the ability to sustain long physical effort

stotting: Keeping hind legs together and front legs together, elk can hop or bounce forward. One theory is that this movement advertises to a predator the good health of the animal. Also, many young ungulates stot when they play. A synonym for stot is pronk.

submissive: allowing others to lead

sulfur: an odorous, combustible non-metal element, which smells like rotten eggs

symbiotic relationship: a relationship between two different organisms that live close together, usually to the benefit of both

talons: the claws of a bird of prey (prey, an animal hunted for food)

terrain: stretch of land

tines: points on an antler

tranquil: quiet, undisturbed

trek: hike

trespassers: those who enter territory without permission

Twenty-one: 21's Crossing: a stony trail north of Soda Butte Creek and east of the Confluence where the creek joins the Lamar River. The famous alpha male of the Druid Peak Pack, Wolf 21, often used the trail to lead hunting parties from the Den Forest on the slope of Druid Peak to the flats along the Lamar River. He was also often observed returning to the den on the same trail, carrying a prize antler or rag of elk skin, toys for his pups. The trail was named to honor him.

ungulates: hoofed mammals, grazers (See stotting for use in a sentence)

vain: without success

vanished: disappeared

veered: changed direction suddenly

vigilant: keeping careful watch for danger

vulnerable: weak and open to attack

wallow: Bison love to roll on the ground. They cover themselves in dust, perhaps to keep insects away, or just to make a big ruckus to show other bison that they are strong and fierce. Often bison use the same spot over and over, creating a bare spot of ground known as a wallow.

warriors: fighters

yowl: a wailing cry of distress

Wolves on the Web

www.bconnollybooks.com (other books by Brian A. Connolly)
www.GeorgeBumann.com
www.wildlifealongtherockies.homestead.com (wildlife photographs)
www.yellowstoneassociation.org (education, books)
www.ypf.org (Yellowstone Park Foundation)
www.yellowstonereports.com
www.mike-oconnell.com
www.markmillerphotos.com (wildlife photographs)
www.lordsofnature.org
www.defenders.org (Defenders of Wildlife)
www.wolf.org (International Wolf Center)
www.nps.gov/yell/naturescience/wolves.htm (Yellowstone Wolves)
www.thewildlifenews.com (search for Kathie Lynch's Yellowstone Wolf Updates)
www.wolftracker.com (wolves, education)
www.tracknature.com
www.trailwoodfilms.com (Bob Landis Wildlife Films)

Brian A. Connolly's novel Wolf Journal was an Oregon Book Award Finalist. A revised German translation of Wolf Journal, Wolftagebuch, was published in Germany in March, 2012. His second novel, Hawk, is the sequel to Wolf Journal. Mr. Connolly writes in Yellowstone and at home in Bend, Oregon. (bconnollybooks.com)

George Bumann is a professional artist and educator in Yellowstone National Park. He lives at the Park's north entrance with his wife, son and two Labradors. His art resides in collections across the U.S. including the Charles Russell Museum in Great Falls, MT & National Museum of Wildlife Art in Jackson, WY. (georgebumann.com)